Twenty-One Years

Based on a True Story

Gee Altaee

Twenty-One Years

Based on a True Story

First edition April 2019; Second edition February 2020.
Book design by Aws Abdullatif

ISBN: 978-0-578-50794-1
Published 97by Gee Altaee
Unites States of America

This novel is dedicated to My Father and to Teresa and Gabby, my editing gurus, and to Aws, who have always loved and supported my dreams.

TABLE OF CONTENTS

Chapter One

Springtime in Michigan can be a delight.

"I've got this one." Jenny posed on one of the short brick pillars at the side of the school's main steps, and she gripped her invisible microphone.

On the main sidewalk below, Sarah held her news- anchor stance. "Over to you, Jenny."

Jenny gestured toward the jock climbing the stairs. "The next star to strut the steps of our Friday Red-Carpet Event here at Bentley High is the fabulous senior..." Jenny adjusted her air microphone, and her long ponytail swished back. "Jay Brookfield. So tell us, Jay, what are your plans for the weekend?" She held the pretend mic under his chin.

He looked unsure of make-believe interview etiquette. "Uh...we've got a track meet in Dearborn, I guess."

"A track meet. All right! Let's hear it for Jay," Jenny yelled. A group of mostly seniors gathered at the bottom of the steps cheered and laughed. Who would be next?

"I'm up," Sarah said. She hopped in constant motion and grabbed her air-microphone again. "Next we have the famous and formidable Julie Cooper, with a voice that doesn't croak like a frog. No, no—it's a silvery voice that made her famous in last year's production of *High   School   Musical.*   Julie, name that song for us, the one with your silvery voice?"

"Silvery   voice?"   Julie   laughed   at   the compliment and looked out at the students waiting for her to answer, as if she was on a real red-carpet runway. "Ahhh... I   guess   "*When   There   Was   Me   and   You*?"

"That's the song. Thank you, Julie. Don't forget us here at Bentley High when you're rich and famous."

"Woot, woot!" The gathering of mostly seniors cheered again with the freedom only a Friday afternoon could inspire.

"And   here   we   have...a   freshman." Jenny twirled in a dance move and extended a hand to the bewildered girl who'd stepped out the school door. "So who are you?"

She leaned closer and pressed her mouth toward Jenny's hand, as if the air-microphone were real. "I'm Ivory, and I'm actually a sophomore."

"Ivory, tell us something about yourself. What are your hopes and dreams? What's your take on world peace? What's your favorite pizza topping?"

Ivory smiled. "Cheese. It's gotta be cheese." "Did you hear that, listeners? Ivory said *cheese*.

Let's make her an honorary junior right now!" "I-vo-ry! I-vo-ry!" The juniors chanted.

Jenny shifted her head, long layers of blond strands swept across her face.

"Now, people, we can't forget about this lovely lady over here," Jenny shouted.

"Samantha, the people want to know, who will you be taking out with you tonight?"

A tall, slender girl, Samantha was hard to miss, though she tried to escape the limelight Jenny had just shone on her.

"It's none of your business," Samantha sputtered in response to Jenny's public prying.

The hordes of high school students that blockaded the bleachers cackled in unison.

"And now, back to you, Friday. This is Jenny—
"

"And Sarah—"

"Signing off." Together they opened their hands and dropped their air-mikes. They bowed with great exaggeration and waved to the pretend crowd of hundreds and to the few dozen real seniors surrounding the stairs.

Jenny had spent every moment of her free time with her cousin Hanna in a hospital room in Ann Arbor, Michigan. They had always been more friends than cousins, but there was something about mini cups of Jello under fluorescent lights that brought them even closer.

Now Jenny's senior year was almost over. And Hanna was gone. Jenny and Sarah had been the last to leave the gravesite.

"Everything happened so fast," Sarah said.

Sarah had been such a good friend. Jenny wiped her cheek again. "Hanna's cancer was aggressive." Jenny had heard her uncle say that, but she didn't see how it helped anything. It was like some monster swooped in. Six weeks, and Hanna was gone forever.

"We should have done something more," Sarah said. "Was there anything else we could have done?"

"Taken her out for one last concert?" Jenny didn't mean to get snarky with Sarah. It wasn't her fault. They followed the narrow, tree-lined path to a waiting car. "We read her favorite books together, gave her makeovers, listened to music, watched movies —"

"And you could always make her laugh," Sarah said. The nurses and doctors at U of M Hospital joked that they learned all the words to *Fargo* just listening to them act out their favorite scenes.

Jenny held a single rose that someone had given her after the service. "Now it's just you and me. Look at everyone from the funeral going back to school or home, going back to their lives. I feel like I'm running in a black-and-white slow-motion movie. I'm running, and I can't get back to where I should be. Don't you dare get sick. Ever. Promise me."

"It's a promise," Sarah said. "But you can't get sick, either." A sudden rain shower made them duck under an oak tree.

Jenny hugged her friend. They clung to each other.

After Hanna's death, Jenny's friends noticed a change. She was always an attractive young lady. Now, however, she entered school with a confidence that electrified the hallways. Suddenly, she had a sharp sense of style that was all her own. She brushed her curly hair until it shone and wore a flower tucked behind her ear every day. Many of the other girls mocked her look, but secretly they were jealous of her.

When she wasn't in class, Jenny enjoyed working with her father. She and her brother Jack, who was a bit older and very overprotective, argued a lot and would fight about everything from the best spot on the sofa to the last piece of cake.

But Jenny loved school. She studied hard and was usually at the top of her class. She had a real fondness for psychology and hoped to major in it when she went away to college. After college, she dreamed of moving to Italy, exploring the city squares in Florence, tasting the limoncello in Sorrento, and strolling the cobbled streets to take in breathtaking vistas of Mt. Vesuvius on the Mediterranean. She longed to see the art museums and study the history of Italy.

After the heartbreak she'd gone through during sophomore year, Jenny had no real interest in boys, no matter how hard they tried to date her or seek a friendship. She had her plan, and boys would surely only get in her way. She'd never let that happen again. Her friend Samantha, on the other hand, had a new crush every week.

One Friday morning before the first bell, Jenny and Samantha stood next to each other gathering their things out of their lockers. Samantha told Jenny, "I really need you to go with me." Jenny had seen this pleading look before. Which guy was it this time? Each guy she brought to meet Jenny was slimier than the last. "There is no way I am going with you on your date."

"I want you there so I don't do something stupid." Samantha slammed her locker door shut.

"Like I can keep you from acting stupid." Jenny closed her locker door and spun the dial on the lock. "What will I do? Sit in the backseat and watch you kiss? Or whatever?" She headed for the stairs.

Samantha ran after her. "I never *whatever* until the third date."

"It's not happening, buttercup." Jenny tried to keep her voice light, but Samantha always tried to make her do stuff she didn't want to do.

Samantha followed Jenny up the wide concrete steps. "Come on Jenny, don't be so mean.

Let's at least go to my house and tell my mother that I'm going home with you to do some homework."

"I knew it," Jenny said. "You just want an alibi.

Again." Jenny told herself this was the last time she was going to let herself be used like this.

Samantha's plan went exactly as she'd wanted, and at 11 p.m. her date dropped her off at Jenny's house. When Samantha didn't come in, Jenny waited 15 minutes then went out to check on her and to meet her mystery man.

His clothes were frayed at the edges and his face was scruffy, like he hadn't used a razor in weeks. Or months. There was something she couldn't figure out about him. Maybe it was his greasy hair. He looked a lot older, too. Samantha had the brains of a half-starved mollusk. What did this guy want with a kid like Samantha, anyway?

Jenny shook her head and strode up to the couple. "So, this is the guy you're dating?" Jenny turned to the stranger. "Where are you from? I haven't seen you around before."

"What? Sam, is this your grandma?" He laughed at his own joke.

But Jenny didn't smile. She didn't back down.

She didn't look away.

"Jenny, this is Moss," Samantha answered.

"I live on the west side," he said. The scowl on his face made it clear he didn't appreciate being interrogated.

"People like Samantha and me don't make time for guys who can't even get cleaned up when they go out on a date. You have to show more respect than that." Jenny headed back to the door. She didn't expect this relationship to last long, so the guy wasn't worth another second of her time.

All the while, Moss stared at her. He couldn't believe all the boys were so interested in Jenny. "She is beautiful. I can't argue that, but what a bitch," he said. "She needs to meet someone who could put her in her place."

Samantha looked a little irritated. Guess he *was* insulting her friend, but she couldn't disagree. The girl thought way too much of herself.

"Like you said, Moss, she thinks she's better than everyone, but it's not you. She treats all the guys like they're lucky to be in her presence."

"Someone really needs to knock her off her high horse. I got someone for her," Moss said.

"You're taking it too serious." Samantha played with the button on his shirt, but he batted her hand away.

"My brother Richard could teach her a lesson." Moss was ready to go. The little bitch had spoiled a perfectly good evening. He reached for the car door handle.

Samantha put her hand on his. "She'd never even look at him," she scoffed. "For starters, he looks too much like you. And he dresses like a homeless guy, even around town."

He knocked her hand away again and jerked the door open. "You don't know him. He can be a nice guy, and if he wants to play the role of an upper-class dude, he could pull it off." He slid in behind the wheel and looked up at her. "He'd love the challenge of showing the princess how wrong it is to look down on people." Moss slammed the door and backed out of the driveway, leaving Samantha standing alone in the dark.

In the house, Samantha found Jenny sitting on her bed.

With a heavy sigh, Samantha flopped down next to her.

Jenny immediately started in. "You know, as soon as I heard his name, I remembered this guy and his family are known for screwing every girl they meet and causing all sorts of trouble. They've even been arrested for drugs and stealing. Don't get involved with him, Sam."

Samantha refused to believe her. "You don't even know him, and you're being so judgey. Just because he doesn't look like everyone else in this town doesn't make him a bad guy. Maybe you should get to know him."

Jenny refused to look up. "I have no interest in getting to know him. I'm only looking out for you. You deserve a guy who has a future."

Samantha stormed out and slammed the door behind her. Insulted and angry that her so-called best friend shamed another boyfriend, she called her mom and said she needed a ride home. While she waited for her mom, she phoned Moss and told him to talk to his brother and get the matchmaking started.

Monday came, and although the day was like any other Monday, Jenny was not herself. Samantha's reactions over the weekend had her feeling down, so she dressed up to disguise her worries. She felt like wearing her hair down and curled around her face with a real rose tucked behind her ear. Her makeup was perfect, as if it was a special occasion, and she was dressed in floating layers that showed off every curve.

She talked Sarah into a walk through downtown Royal Oak.

"Samantha did it again," Jenny said. "She had me cover for her while she went out with the worst possible guy in town."

Sarah shook her head. "Who was it this time?" "A guy named Moss; he's from the west side."

"My dad used to take our car to their family's shop, but he only did a few times," Sarah said. "I don't know why he stopped. Something about ripping him off.

"I think there's a couple brothers, maybe a sister? They're kind of a mob family. Samantha really should stay away," Sarah said.

"That's what I said. Sarah, you should have seen this guy the other night."

Walking down the busy street, Jenny made Sarah laugh by imitating Moss and his personality, comparing him to a three-toed sloth in a Mustang.

At the corner, a car passed by, and Jenny looked at the driver. He made eye contact with her. "Did you see the guy in that car?" Jenny asked. "Oh my gosh, he was so handsome, and that car was amazing."

"No, I really wasn't paying attention," Sarah said.

Jenny felt her face flush. They walked a little farther and Jenny caught herself daydreaming about coming face- to-face with the handsome driver of the shiny BMW.

Jenny shrieked, "Oh my God, he's coming back. He turned around." She was startled back into reality. "I'm being crazy. He's probably lost. But how do I look?"

"You look great," Sarah whispered. "Just don't get nutty."

The car pulled over to the side of the road. The guy slid out of the BMW and strolled toward them. He ran his hand through his dark tousled hair, which was a little longer than she was used to. There was something familiar about his green eyes that were focused only on her. Even up close, he was incredibly attractive. He approached the girls and held out his hand to Jenny in a gentlemanly handshake.

He leaned down toward her ear adorned with the rose. "Jenny Alan? You've changed so much since the last time I saw you. Do you know how pretty you are?" he said softly.

Jenny wasn't sure how to respond. She reached out and took his hand. His handshake was strong and solid. "I've heard that a lot," she said.

If she had met him before, she couldn't remember. The puzzled look on her face tipped him off.

"You don't remember me? I'm Michael. Michael Anderson," he said.

Jenny's mind raced to think of something flirty or clever to say. "Hi Michael," she said, still holding his hand. "I know that guy sitting on the bench over there more than I know you." She pointed to a man feeding bread to giddy pigeons. "You look a little familiar," she conceded. So much for flirty or clever. It could be a job interview. She couldn't think straight.

"This is Sarah, my best friend," she added, introducing the two strangers.

Michael let go of Jenny's hand and greeted Sarah. Together, they walked the short distance to the corner coffee shop. Michael motioned toward the door and invited them inside, where they went to a two-seat table in the back. Michael asked Sarah if she would mind leaving the two of them to talk.

This guy was kind of bold. Jenny gave Sarah the nod.

Sarah took a seat at the counter about ten feet away.

A server brought Michael a coffee and a little silver cream pitcher and then took Jenny's coffee order. Jenny and Michael sat in silence for a few moments. She wasn't sure what to say. She usually shut guys down before things got this far, but she couldn't stop staring at his eyes. She had no room in her life for boys, but this guy was no boy. And those eyes. "So, you told Sarah you wanted to have a word with me, yet you've said nothing."

Michael smiled. "I'm finding myself speechless looking at this goddess in front of me."

Jenny blushed like crazy and decided she would be the one to strike up a true conversation. Flattery is wonderful, but she really wanted to get to know this guy. She asked where he was from and was surprised that it was not far from her home. Birmingham, Michigan is not that big.

They both talked about their family businesses in town. Jenny wondered if she had met him before.

"But we have," Michael said. "My dad's construction company has worked with your dad's landscape company. I've seen you in the office working, but back then you wore t-shirts and jeans with grass stains. I never expected this." He waved his hand up and down like he was a game show host showing off the prize behind door number three.

Jenny laughed. "That's why you looked familiar." Why hadn't she noticed him before?

"Your dad had some great ideas and lots of experience. I remember him when I used to go with my father to his office. I was young back then."

Jenny was pleased that he respected her dad.

After a short while, Michael cleared his throat and said, "Would you consider going out and doing something with me?"

"Do something? Like what?"

"Dinner or a movie. I'd like to take you on a date," he said. "Dinner and a movie, perhaps?"

"With or without popcorn?"

"Extra butter and a box of Goobers."

She scooted her chair back. "I'll think about it."

Michael laughed. "No. You don't get to think about it. You only get to say *yes*."

Jenny laughed and stood. "You sound like a crazy guy."

Michael stood. "You have no idea." He handed her his business card. "Call me, and we'll make plans."

Jenny smiled as she read the card with his business name on it. She was impressed that someone his age carried a business card. Jenny looked at the card again and then back at him. "You're Michael Anderson."

"Yes, I believe I told you that." He grinned, and boy, were his teeth white. And straight.

"It's all starting to ring a bell now, even my brother Jack knows you," Jenny said.

"Nice job." Michael laughed. "Jack's little sister sure has grown up."

"I know, he doesn't look anything like me. Also, my sense of humor is far superior." Jenny tried to keep a straight face.

"In fact, I was planning to visit Jack later this evening.

That will give me a chance to see you again."

This was too much, too fast for Jenny. She looked around for Sarah.

Michael quickly changed the subject. "This is a busy time of year for your family, isn't it?"

"I have to go now. Sarah is waiting for me. Thanks for the coffee. It was very nice to meet you."

She could feel Michael watching as she walked away.

For the rest of the day, Jenny could not stop talking about Michael. She rambled on for what seemed like forever about Michael's family and their very well-known construction business. She raved about his striking appearance and how kind-hearted he seemed. Sarah mentioned that Jenny had never shown this much interest in a boy before.

When Michael got home and found his mother in the kitchen, he hugged her and kissed her on the cheek.

His mother looked at him with a curious frown. "Why are you so happy?"

"Mom, I'm the luckiest guy alive right now," he said. "Have you ever seen a goddess? I met one. She's so beautiful, it's almost like she's a dream. She wears a rose behind her ear." His

mom listened intently.

"Remember Jack Alan? He's been over a few times. The Alans, they live close by. It's his younger sister, the goddess. So grown up now and beautiful beyond belief."

Later that evening, Michael called Jenny's house and was thrilled to hear her voice again. Unfortunately, she cut him short. She said she had too much homework to do to see him, almost as if playing hard to get. He told her that he missed her.

But she said he was crazy to miss someone he'd just met and hung up.

Michael was a little hurt at first, but he liked feisty, and he was even more determined to pursue Jenny, though she was apparently going to be difficult.

Several times over the next few days, Michael tried to set up a date. Finally, he had enough of being rejected. He wasn't sure if she was being rude to see how long he would keep chasing her or if she truly wasn't interested.

A week had passed when Michael knocked on the front door. Jenny and her mother were preparing dinner, and when she opened the door and found him there, her breath caught in her throat. "I wasn't expecting you," she said.

"Hello to you, too. I came to see Jack," he said.

"He's not here, and I'm making dinner," she said.

"Then I'll see you instead." Michael smiled. "I'd be glad to join you for dinner."

Jenny shook her head. "I don't think so." She shut the door.

Michael was left stunned, but smiling. This girl was really going to be difficult.

When Jenny returned to the kitchen, her mother asked who was at the door. Jenny shrugged and told her it was one of Jack's friends. She shook her hands as if she were trying to dry them and went back to cooking. There was some confusion in her mind. Did she make the right decision? Should she have invited him for dinner? It might've been fun. She found herself being extra careful cutting onions to make sure the knife didn't slip in her trembling hands.

The next day at school, Samantha and Jenny were cordial to each other, but they were both noticeably irritated. It was clear that Samantha still harbored some grudge against Jenny, although Jenny couldn't understand why. She could only help a friend so much if they refused to change.

On the way home, as they were about to part ways, Samantha stopped walking. "I need to stop by later today."

"Again? Who is it this time?" Jenny asked. "Who do you think?" Samantha said.

Jenny's voice hardened. "I would guess that you have another date with that ape man from the west side."

"You are so mean," Samantha screamed.

Jenny knew she was being mean, but it was warranted. She had been noticing new things about Samantha. In class, she was more frenzied, always tapping her pencil in ways she had never done before. She only wore long sleeved shirts now. Jenny suspected drugs, likely from her lowlife boyfriend, Moss. But she'd kept her mouth shut on that matter.

Jenny held her hand up like a traffic cop stopping cars. "I'm not in the mood to put up with this nonsense today.

You don't want to hear what I have to say, anyway. I know what I know, and you are so blind you can't listen to anyone."

Samantha explained that she wanted Jenny to meet Moss's brother. He was a nice guy, and they could double date. Jenny tried not to hurt her feelings again, but she had too much schoolwork to double date. "Besides," she said, "I've kind of got my eye on someone else." She could see Samantha was very curious.

"But Moss is my boyfriend *now*."

Samantha tried one last time. "At least think about it."

Jenny shook her head. "Your boyfriend. I'm not interested. His family are filthy people. What if they kidnap you? You could be raped. I just do not trust them."

"Well, first off," Samantha said, "they aren't like that. And second he's—it wouldn't be rape." She put her head down and blushed.

Jenny shook her head. "Don't you have any boundaries?"

"He's the best," Samantha said. "We are so in love."

"You are so cheap. How could you do something like that? And with him?"

"How dare you call me cheap? Where do you get off judging me? Sex is sex," said Samantha.

"You should be waiting for someone special who loves you. It means something to me. Obviously, not to you." Jenny sashayed off and left Samantha fuming.

Samantha was so furious she called Moss. This was the worst breech in their friendship ever, and Jenny would pay. She agreed that they needed to meet with his brother Richard and describe what they wanted him to do.

Samantha's first impression of Moss's brother was how strange he was. He ran his fingers through his greasy hair, which was pasted to his face. Moss had left out the part about his brother's serious mental issues. They sat on the floor of Moss's room, taking turns with the hypodermic needle. The more meth they injected, the more passionate their complaints against Jenny became.

Richard listened to the two of them talk about how mean Jenny was. They wanted Richard to meet her and work his way into her life. Once she had fallen for him, they hoped he would be able to teach her a lesson about how dangerous it is to judge someone by what he appeared to be. Richard being charming and kind was the furthest thing from the truth.

Samantha could see Richard's eyes alight with schemes to carry out their plan. He seemed to find this prank intriguing, almost entertaining. Moss and Samantha might have just unleashed a monster. But as mad as Samantha was, she was okay with that. And as she slipped into a drug induced sleep, she felt content with her decision to wage revenge on Jenny.

Jenny walked with Sarah at the park near school.

Michael followed them in his car and waited for Sarah to leave. When Jenny was by herself, Michael parked and set off walking toward her. When he finally caught up with her, he grabbed her arm and twirled her around to show off his best smile. "I've been trying to get in touch with you," he said.

Jenny apologized for ignoring his calls. "Look I'm getting ready for a string of exams. After that we can talk about everything. I have to focus on school right now," she said.

Michael wasn't the type to accept being put off. He frowned and said, "I don't think it has anything to do with exams. I think you're just giving me a hard time. I think you enjoy the chase, and that's fine. But sooner or later, the chase has to end so the real fun can begin."

Jenny finally stopped walking and looked him in the eye. "Okay then, what is it you want?"

His frown softened. "I want to go somewhere to talk. I want to get to know you. There's a café around the corner."

At the café, they sat at a small table and sipped their coffee. Michael made fun of Jenny's drink choice. Sugar- free vanilla latte with an espresso shot and extra foam. He chuckled under his breath. There was no real conversation, just staring and uncomfortable silence.

Finally, Jenny pushed Michael to find out what his intentions were with asking her to come here. Obviously, it wasn't to talk.

Michael explained that he wanted to go on a real date, and that he was hoping for a real relationship with her. He was very honest about his feelings for her and told her that she hurt him with her rejections. "You are making me crazy." He laughed.

Jenny laughed at him at first, but when she saw that he was being sincere, she realized that she may really be hurting his feelings, and she got serious. "Okay," she said, "I'll make you a deal. You leave me alone until after my exams are over, and I promise we will go on a date. Then, we can see where things go from there." She drank her coffee down to the bottom and put the cup back on the table with a decisive bump. It felt like a fair compromise.

"It's a deal," Michael agreed with a wink. He kissed her hand, stood, and headed back to his car.

When her exams were over, Jenny was relieved and much more relaxed. She had begun to check into some scholarship opportunities and was applying to in-state universities. She'd been saving money for a long time, but the schools that specialized in psychology and housing in the areas of those schools, were very expensive.

Scholarships would be really helpful. At the same time, she was distracted thinking about Michael and what she had promised him. She tried to convince herself that she was only agreeing to a date because she'd promised, but deep down, she wanted to see him.

Michael had arranged to take her to a romantic Italian restaurant downtown. They walked in, and the host seated them in a cozy corner booth. They peeked over the tall menus at one another.

"I'm so glad we finally got to do this," Michael said. "I've been waiting a long time. You know, before we met, I had my heart set on a beautiful girl like you to fall in love with, settle down, and get married. Then, like a wish come true, there you were."

Jenny gasped. "What? Have you become unbalanced? Flipped out? Have you gone berserk?"

"I told you. I want a real relationship, love, and marriage. The whole thing." He looked totally innocent.

Jenny felt sudden butterflies and wondered how she could eat dinner. Her hands fluttered as she tried to convince him that it was way too early to think about such things. They had not even started their lives yet. "We haven't seen the world. We haven't experienced anything. We all have our own ideas about our lives, and it's different for everyone. I can't think about what you're saying until I graduate college. And even then, I want to travel." She waited for his reaction.

He wasn't laughing, only listening.

She softened her voice. "I've always wanted to live in Italy for a while."

"We can do that together," he said. "But tell me why you'd want to leave your family and your country to go all the way to Italy."

"Are you really living if you aren't exploring? Are you really growing if you aren't seeing what else is out there and learning from people that don't look like you and places you aren't familiar with?" Jenny explained. "I want to travel because everywhere here, where we're at right now, looks the same for me. I have dreams to see more and be more." She folded her napkin and set it on the table. "Can we go now?"

Jenny made some time for Michael, but spent most of her time studying and hanging out with her friends from school. This didn't make Michael happy, but he accepted it, because it made her happy.

The next Friday, Jenny was invited to a party at her friend's house. Even though the house was huge, it was still crowded with people. Sarah was excited to introduce her friend Oliver to Jenny. He was very nice boy, who loved music and played guitar. He was short and had long hair. He seemed well liked by everyone, probably because he was so friendly. Sarah knew Jenny would like him.

Sarah grabbed Oliver's hand and walked him over to where Jenny stood by the buffet and introduced them to each other.

Sarah walked away, and Jenny and Oliver kept talking, getting to know each other. Oliver went to get a mix CD from his car for Jenny. She was interested in the songs he'd written. While she waited for him to come back, she got in line to get another drink. Another guy came up behind her and handed her a drink with a smile. She took the glass and thanked him. As she started to walk away, he stepped in front of her.

"Hello, beautiful. I'm Richard." He held out his free hand. "Please don't think I'm rude, but I cannot stop staring at you. You are truly the most beautiful girl I've ever seen."

Jenny tried to be polite, but she'd heard that line her whole life—even when she was a little girl. "Well, that's very nice of you to say...excuse me." Jenny felt very uncomfortable, so she headed out the door to get some air.

As she walked down the stairs, she saw Michael's car pull up across the street. He got out of the driver's side, and a tall, muscular guy got out of the passenger seat. They jogged across the street. Richard was watching her through the huge bay window. Men were so weird.

Michael finally caught her eye, "Jenny, I'm so happy to see you here."

She smiled. "Sarah invited me; apparently she invited the whole city."

"This is my good friend James," Michael said. "He worked at my dad's construction company."

Jenny smiled up at the handsome giant, and he grinned back. "I've heard a lot about you," he said.

She shot Michael a look that could wither an oak tree. "Not just from Michael," James said. "Although, I don't think Michael has talked about anyone or anything else since he met you, goddess."

"It's freezing, why are you out here?" Michael took her hand. "Let's get inside."

"I just walked out. It's so crowded inside, and there was a strange man. I didn't feel comfortable and just wanted to get away for a minute."

"What did he do to you?" Michael snapped.

"Nothing. He was just acting weird. Like, over friendly."

"Where is he? I'll beat his ass," said Michael. He sounded ferocious.

She liked that he wanted to protect her, but was a little taken aback by how mad he got. "I get that you want to protect me, but really, it's fine."

Michael stood there smiling. He wrapped his jacket around her shoulders. "So, have you thought about a real date yet?"

"Quite possibly. She smiled, but not till after graduation," Jenny said.

Michael opened the door for her. "And the chase continues."

"No, I'm not looking to be chased. I just have a plan." She poked his arm. "Didn't you ever want to go to college?"

"I thought about it, but I went to work in my family business when I was really young. I kind of learned as I went along. No regrets though. It's a good business, and I'm very good at it—if I do say so myself."

He took her arm gently and leaned down for a kiss.

Jenny stepped back and told him that her first kiss had to be special. "It should be somewhere else and not at a time like this. Not in public. Even the music is crazy here."

"I get it, but at least you didn't say *never*." They went back in and spent the whole night together with friends enjoying the party.

A few days later, Richard had a plan to get Jenny's attention. It was clear that simple flattery at house parties was not going to work. So he rode his motorcycle to the area he knew she'd be walking. When she approached, he hit the brakes and flipped his bike, making it look like an accident.

She saw the bike flip and skid across the street. He looked like a rag doll as he flopped over the front of the bike. She pulled out her phone and rushed to the driver lying on the cement. Behind the helmet, his eyes were tiny, sharp darts that pierced through her when she asked if he was okay. The man groaned and held his arm.

She started to dial 911, but the man reached up urgently. Jenny slipped the phone into her pocket and offered him her hand. He took it and sat up on the ground. In a swift motion, he took off his helmet.

She realized she'd met him before, but she couldn't remember where. She pulled out the phone and started to dial 911 again, but he quickly assured her he'd be okay. It was sure too bad about his bike, though.

He struggled to get to his feet, certainly playing it up for her sympathy, went to his motorcycle and stood it up. He put his helmet on the bike and walked back to her. "I think I'm good, just a little banged up is all. Thank you for your help; I appreciate it."

He invited Jenny out for a drink to thank her for her kindness, but she made her excuses and left him standing in the road. Richard felt he had his foot in the door as he watched her leave. Now he just wondered what his next play should be.

Over the next few days, he gathered a lot of information about Jenny from her friend Samantha. She told him what Jenny liked and what she was planning to do with her life. From her desire to travel to her bubbly personality and way of looking at life through a humorous lens, he learned enough about her that his plan became clear.

Jenny spent her weekends either partying or going out with her friends. Sarah always joined Jenny, but Samantha had been MIA for a while. Sarah and Jenny had seen Samantha and Moss around town a few times, looking frail and buzzed out. Jenny worried, but realized there was nothing she could say or do.

She continued to live her life. At parties, Sarah and Jenny loved to dance. A few times, Jenny had run into Michael just by chance. He was charming, and she was resistant. They had casual conversations, and she thought he was gorgeous. She spent a lot time with Oliver. He was the guy everyone hired to play music at their parties, so she saw him everywhere. He was sweet and funny, and he and Jenny liked the same things. They had the same taste in music, movies, and food. They loved to eat. Richard was at a few of the parties, but she really didn't pay much attention to him.

At one party, Richard noticed that Michael wasn't there. Oliver was busy playing music. Richard hated Oliver and Michael. They stood between him and Jenny. He saw this as his chance to approach her again. She was dancing with her friends, having a great time. They made eye contact, and he waved at her. She returned the gesture and turned away. When she went to get a drink, he waited for her to walk past. "Good to see you, Jenny." He smiled.

"Hi, good to see you, too," she said.

"You dance beautifully," he said.

"Why aren't you dancing?" she asked, shouting over the loud music.

He shook his head no.

Jenny was confused. "Why? Didn't you come to have fun?"

Richard acted like he couldn't hear and motioned to the door. They went out into the hallway where it was quieter. Richard went on to explain that he didn't join in because he felt out of place. He told her that people only invite him to make fun of him. He was paranoid and figured that because he wasn't rich like everyone else in town, and he wasn't as handsome as some of the others, that everyone was against him.

She asked him why he came to the parties if he really felt that way, and he explained that he was very lonely at home. Jenny felt bad for him, consoled him, and reassured him that not everyone there was rich and good looking. She told him that being yourself is the key to making friends.

Richard changed the subject. "So, I hear you plan to go away to college?"

Jenny said, "Yes. I want to study Psychology."

Richard's eyes widened. "Wow, what a coincidence. I love psychology."

"Is that what you majored in?" Jenny asked.

Richard shook his head. "No, I never went to college, but I like it. I read some books about it. I'm into books and history."

Jenny realized that they had been away for quite a while, opened the door, and went back inside. Richard seemed very pleased with himself, but she didn't know why.

A couple months later, Jenny's college acceptance letters finally came in, and she received the news she'd been waiting for. Jenny's family threw her a huge party to celebrate her getting into the university of her dreams.

Everything was coming together just the way she wanted it to.

She was surprised to see Michael when she opened the door. He smiled his sweet smile and handed her a small giftwrapped box. "Thank you," she said. "How sweet of you."

Michael waited to be let in when Jenny asked, "Who invited you?"

Michael was caught off guard. "Jack invited me. You didn't, but Jack did."

"I'm sorry, I didn't mean to be..."

"You're still treating me like shit, and I'm doing everything to make you happy." Then, he turned and left.

She stood at the door, speechless. She spent the rest of the evening unhappy. She was too harsh with Michael. She really didn't intend to hurt his feelings.

Chapter Two

The summer before college passed quickly. Jenny worked in her father's office at the landscape company by day and packed boxes in her room at night. On one side of the room were boxes for a move to the new family home in Bloomfield Hills. On the other side were boxes for her college dorm room.

In August, the moving van came and upended her childhood home. Gone was her collection of porcelain dolls from around the world. Only an empty shelf remained. She checked her brother's room to see if their blanket was still there.

Under his bed they hid an oversized blanket to be pulled out when they wanted to make a castle, a fort, or a tent. Draped over chairs and a footstool, it made a perfect childhood hideout on a rainy day for playing card games or making up stories to scare each other. But the mattress was stacked against the wall ready for the movers.

They were no longer children, but Jenny loved the idea of the blanket still there under Jack's bed. She hated this change. Why did they have to move right now when she was trying to survive the leap from high school to college?

The move didn't take them far from their old neighborhood, and her father's company had planted new landscaping with berms, swales, and gingko trees. He had asked her advice, and she noticed a few of the perennial flowers she'd suggested at the corner under her bedroom window. On a walk around the house, she couldn't help but see that the sprinkler system wasn't reaching her flowers. Jenny made a mental note to tell her father, and she pulled a watering can from a box in the garage.

She was watering her new plants in the front yard when she saw Michael pull up the drive. He walked up, and as soon as he saw the garden hose, he picked it up and sprayed Jenny from top to bottom. She squealed from the shock of cold water, and her watering can flew from her hand. She ran behind him to grab a length of the garden hose and wrestle it away, so she could return the favor, atomizing the spray to reduce him to a dripping mass.

"How can I go back to work like this?" Michael looked down at his drenched shirt and pants. "I get no phone call. I finally track you down, and this is how you greet me," he teased.

"Oh yeah, well look at me." Jenny pulled at her wet t-shirt. "We just moved in, and I'm unpacking this place that will never feel like home, and I still have boxes waiting to go to the dorm at college. I've been more than a little tied up. I know you find this hard to believe, but you really weren't the first thing on my mind." Jenny's demeanor was snippy and playful at the same time.

Just then, Jack pulled into the driveway. When he joined them in the front yard, he seemed surprised to see Michael. Jack looked at the two of them, but didn't ask why they were standing there soaking wet. "Hey, this new grass is getting pretty soggy, Jen. You want to turn this thing off?" he said.

Jenny left them, and Jack looked at his friend. "How about those Tigers?" Michael said.

"I need to talk to you, and it's not about the Tigers," Jack said.

Jack motioned to Michael to come inside with him. As much as Jack wrangled with his little sister, he still wanted what was best for her. He was curious about Michael's interest.

"I assure you, I'm thinking long term here, but your sister has yet to accept even a date with me. I've been patient, but I can only wait so long."

Jack appreciated Michael's honesty, but warned his friend that he had better be careful not to hurt her. He gave Michael a slap on his wet back. "I know you, dude; I know what kind of guy you are." It almost implied that Michael had his blessing.

Michael walked to his car and saw Jenny still tending the plants. He gave her a wave over his shoulder. "Soon," he shouted as he climbed into the car. He slammed the door and peeled away. He sure did look good in that car.

Jack came back outside and looked at her. She stood and brushed dirt from her knees. "What? What are you looking at? He only came here looking for you."

Jack chuckled. "Yep, that's why right after he called me and I told him I wasn't home, he came to see *me*?"

Jenny picked up a fistful of soil and pelted her brother.

Over the summer months, Jenny and Oliver became very close friends. They were happy that Sarah had introduced them. Now that fall classes had started, Jenny was pleased that Oliver's house was close to campus, so when she had breaks, she would go to his place to hang out and study.

With her focus on college, she didn't worry too much about making time to see Michael, even after his efforts to set up a date with her. That guy was way too serious too soon.

With Oliver, there was no pretense, no expectation. He didn't constantly ogle over her beauty. Oliver treated her like a human being with something to offer outside of her looks. They talked about actualization and Maslow's hierarchy of needs: physiological, safety, love and belonging, esteem, and self-actualization.

"I think I feel pretty good about myself, but I'm not quite where I want to be at, you know?" Jenny said one day while listening to Oliver's latest mixes.

"It's all a process, Jenny. Don't they teach you that in your psych classes?" he joked. "Anyways, it seems like it probably takes people a long time to be self-actualized or whatever."

Science didn't really interest him as much as notes and melodies. But Jenny enjoyed their almost daily conversations. Talking with Oliver was like breathing. It was routine.

At Oliver's house one afternoon, Jenny felt a tension that she hadn't felt before. It was a crisp fall day, and they sat in his backyard. He was playing his guitar and she was reading, sipping cold apple cider. Oliver stopped playing and told Jenny that he needed to tell her something. "I'm worried that you'll be upset by what I have to say," he began.

This heightened her tension. What could he possibly say that would upset her? He was the kindest guy she'd ever met. She smiled and tried to make light of it. "Just say it. Don't be silly, what is it?"

"I love you," he whispered.

Jenny laughed and smacked him playfully. "I love you, too, my dear. You and Sarah are my dearest friends."

"No," Oliver reached over and put his hand on her knee. "I mean, I think I'm in love with you."

Jenny pushed his hand away and laughed again. "What's in this cider? Are you drunk?" Her smile was gone, replaced by panic.

Oliver searched her eyes. "I'm not thinking of Sarah, I want you. Can't you tell? You come over here in the afternoons, and when you leave, I can't wait until you're back beside me again. I—"

"Oh, Oliver." Jenny's eyes brimmed with tears. "You know I adore you. Why would we risk our perfect friendship? Things are wonderful the way they are. I just can't do this right now... I want you to always be my friend—not more than that, please. I've lost people in my life and had so many changes. You and Sarah are the best friends I've ever had, and I don't want to lose you, too."

Oliver sighed. He set his guitar aside and hugged her. "I hoped what I said would make you happy, but now I have to apologize for upsetting you." His hands rested on her shoulders, and then slowly dropped to his sides in defeat. "I promise we will always be friends. Nothing can stop that, ever." He tried to smile.

Jenny felt awful. "What if I told you that I already love someone? I mean, I'm in love with someone."

Oliver sighed. "I would envy him. Do I know him?"

Jenny looked at Oliver. "I'm in love with Michael," she admitted. Hearing herself say it out loud gave her goose bumps, and she rubbed her arms.

Oliver nodded. "I should've known." He looked serious. "I mean, I knew he loved you. I've seen the way he looks at you and the way he talks to you. I knew it."

Jenny said, "Michael is a good man, but I don't know if I'm good for him. I have things that I want to do before I get serious with anyone. We both have dreams. I don't want him to change for me, but I'm not giving up my dreams, either. I'm scared. What if we gave up so much that we ended up hating each other? I can't believe I'm telling you this, Oliver, after what you just told me. It must hurt to hear it, but you're my friend, and I want to know what you think."

"Does he know you love him?" asked Oliver.

"I think he does, but you know how I am. I can be a pretty tough nut to crack," she said.

"Jenny, he really loves you. Tell him you're conflicted, but tell him how you feel. You may want different things right now, but you don't know what will happen in the future. You need to live your life, and you can't make him happy unless you're happy, too."

Jenny could tell Oliver wanted what was best for her.

Maybe he had caught on to the self-actualization thing, after all.

Jenny thought a lot about what Oliver told her. She decided to meet Michael and go out on a real date with him. She had put life's priorities ahead of relationships long enough. If Michael had waited for her all this time, that said a lot about him, and she was ready.

Wearing a new outfit and a little yellow rose in her hair, Jenny waited for Michael on the sidewalk in front of her dorm. He pulled over and got out to open the car door for her. He stood close to her and kissed her hand. "You are a goddess. You look stunning."

"And you—" Jenny paused to check out his look: casual, yet eye-catching. "You're not wearing any socks." She couldn't get herself to compliment him.

"I thought you might melt at the sight of my bare ankles, and you'd be mine forever."

Jenny thought she might, but she wasn't going to let him know that.

Jenny slipped into the seat next to him. The new leather interior was impressive. She fiddled with the dials until he finally hit a button that brought Bruce Springsteen through the speakers in surround sound.

Michael put her at ease from the moment she sat in his car. And they went to a restaurant they both liked. At the cozy corner table, they spoke about her college classes and Michael's work with

45

the family business before Michael touched on the question she knew he really wanted to ask. "What made you decide to go out on a real date with me?"

Jenny smiled. "I didn't change my mind, but like I told you before, there had to be a right time for it."

"Well it took you long enough," he teased. "Years. A big part of our lives has passed." She raised her glass of wine, as if to toast him. "And no doubt, it was worth the wait," she said.

"In fact, you gave me so much time to wait, I worked on a little project for you," Michael mentioned. "Wanna see it later?"

Jenny had no idea what he could be up to, but her curiosity got the best of her. "Sure, why not?" she said.

After dinner, Jenny and Michael drove around the city. They talked and joked and ended up in a makeshift gravel driveway, bumping along to a stop. Jenny looked up to see a castle-like home. The house looked like a palace. "Is it your house?" Jenny asked. "It's incredible."

Michael stepped out of the car and opened the door for her.

Jenny looked at the imposing height and one of-a-kind features. "What is it they say about the frame of a solid house? It has good bones," she said.

"I'll take that compliment. I designed it," Michael said. "I built this house for you, Jenny. For us."

"Built it for us?"

"Exactly," he confirmed. "When I started to think about you seriously, I wasted no time. We'll live here together when we get married. This is the project I've been working on. Your surprise." Michael took Jenny's hand and led her to the ground floor study. It was elaborate with matching mahogany desks and chairs. She took a seat in one while Michael poured them both a glass of wine.

"I've waited so long for this day, Jenny," Michael said. "Time was passing by without me feeling it," Jenny replied.

"Well, what do you think of the place?" Michael asked.

"I'm so impressed with what you created, truly." She couldn't describe the tsunami of emotions hitting her all at once. She just took in every piece of her surroundings. He had done this for her.

"After graduation, could you see yourself living here, with me, and being married?"

Oh Michael, still impatient, still refusing to acknowledge her dreams to travel, work, and live a big, full life. "Michael, you know I can't promise you that. I'm young, and I haven't done even half of the things I want to do," Jenny said.

Instead of responding with words, Michael simply pulled a small red box out of his pocket. He opened it to reveal a sparkling, gold ring with a diamond centerpiece. Jenny held out her hand instinctively, and he slipped it on her finger.

"I don't know how long it will take for you to live out your dreams, but I will wait for you. I love you and want you for the rest of my life, no matter what that takes. I want you to marry me."

Michael is too good and too understanding. Jenny was speechless, and her eyes filled with tears. Even after rejecting him—again—he was asking her to marry him.

He placed his hands on either side of her cheeks, using his palms to dry the tears that rolled down her face.

He leaned over and barely touched her lips; a preview of what might come next. And then he kissed her with a passion unleashed from years of waiting. Jenny felt the warmth of his body in an electric moment beyond reason or explanation.

He stood back to look at her. She searched for words to explain. "Michael, you waited so long. Why didn't you tell me it would be like this? Why did I wait so long?"

He embraced her, and again, she felt his intensity and warmth. "Could we just stay like this? I don't want to leave."

"Soon," Michael said. "But first, I want you, all of you. Let's go to the bedroom."

Together, Jenny and Michael ascended the spiral stairway leading to the master bedroom. Michael pushed the door open, hardly able to contain his excitement. He'd waited a long time for this very moment.

He flipped a switch, and the ceiling transformed into a night sky. There were stars amid the blackness. Jenny, mesmerized, gasped at the sight. Michael motioned toward the bed, where they now stood gazing at each other in the soft light.

"I'm in love with you, Jenny," Michael announced. "I will show you just how much you mean to me."

"Prove it to me," Jenny said with a sly smile. She wanted him, all of him, too.

While tracing each curve of Jenny's body with his eyes and hands, Michael slowly unbuttoned his shirt.

Seeing his body for the first time took her breath away. He lifted her up, twirled her around as if they were dancing, and placed her on the bed. He called her his goddess. He kissed her neck, and then his lips worked their way down her body, slowly, as if they had all the time in the world.

By the time he got to her belly, she couldn't stand the exquisite wait anymore. She whispered in his ear, "I love you, and I want you now."

Jenny loved his strength and the way he moved inside her body. She lost all control. She pulled at his back and didn't realize that she'd scratched him with her nails until later that evening—after they'd made love so many times she lost count. Satisfied, they fell asleep in each other's arms.

That Saturday morning, the bright sun filled the bedroom and woke Jenny. She saw that the balcony door was open, and she knew Michael was out there. She wrapped herself in the bed sheet and tiptoed out to join him.

Michael kissed her forehead. "Good morning, my love."

"Good morning," she whispered.

"How did you sleep? I hope last night wasn't too rough for you."

Jenny felt embarrassed. Michael seemed to have an endless store of creative ways to make love. When she dozed off last night, she felt both exhausted and exhilarated. "I'm fine. I feel good. Everything was perfect."

Michael sat next to her on the balcony and took her hand. "I know this is all so new to you. I'm truly the luckiest man in the world."

Jenny laid her head on his shoulder. "You're the only one I ever wanted to be with," she said.

They talked again about how soon "soon" was. Michael was conflicted between his desire to marry soon or to accept Jenny's wishes to graduate and accomplish her own dreams in Europe. "You'll know when it's the right time," he told her.

"What if I'm not really the right woman for you? You know I love you, but sharing my dreams with you would take you away from the life you've made here for yourself. In time you'd end up resenting me."

They argued the point for a while until Michael finally decided he'd heard enough. He lifted her up into his arms, carried her back into the rumpled bed, and gently made love to her again.

A week later, Jenny had coffee with Sarah. Everything about Michael tumbled out at once. "He's in love with me, Sarah. I do love him, too. I'm so lightheaded, and I can't think of anything else."

"I figured by looking at you," Sarah said. "So tell." "Tell what, silly?" Jenny said.

"Jenny! So you finally did it. So, what now?" Sarah asked.

"I think I finally realized I love him, and I told him that I love him. It felt right to be with him, you know?"

"Of course. Jen, you are making up for years of waiting. Was it what you thought it would be?"

"It was more than what I could have ever imagined," Jenny exclaimed. "He surprised me with a house. He built it for me. Who does that?"

Sarah's jaw nearly hit the floor. The level of commitment this guy had was unheard of these days.

"What if I'm not good for him? What if he only thinks he loves me, but he just loves the way I look? How do I know he loves me when he calls me a goddess? I just don't know, Sarah."

Jenny sipped her coffee. "There's so much more to loving someone than what we see. It's all so confusing."

"Don't overthink this, psych major," Sarah said. "Enjoy the ride."

It really was quite a ride.

Jenny worked tirelessly to make the Dean's List, and some semesters, the President's List. Her friendships grew, even among students she tutored. She would stop to ask professors questions after class, and they would send her books to read, sometimes months after she'd been in their class. She appreciated their encouragement and wanted to do well for them as well as for herself.

One morning, she chose a seat near the back of the 300-seat hall of her abnormal psych class. Tired from a night of studying, she pulled her laptop from her backpack. A tall, lanky basketball type slipped into the seat next to her.

The professor said, "Remember the four Ds: deviance, dysfunction, distress, danger as they may represent..."

She tapped notes in a rapid beat to this strange, fascinating language. Lanky leaned over. His quick and casual patter kept up as she struggled to listen to the professor.

"Really," she said to him. "I don't know this stuff. I have to listen." She kept typing.

"Disturbing behavior may be emotional, cognitive, and or behavioral. For example..."

Lanky was in the middle of talking about his party that weekend. She'd had enough. She snapped her laptop, grabbed her backpack, and sidestepped past classmates to the first empty seat she could find.

"Fuuu—ck you, Cowboy Princess," he called after her.

Her face felt hot. She looked down at her boots. Her dad had given them to her after a business trip to Texas, and she loved them.

She glanced down at the ring Michael had given her. Would she ever feel confident enough to keep it on her finger?

Later that day during lunch in the campus café, Jenny glanced up and saw Richard approaching. She was shocked to see him there. She jumped out of her seat in front of him. "Richard...what are you doing here?" Jenny's voice was abrupt.

"I'm here to visit a friend. Never thought I'd run into you. How have you been?"

"My brain has been taken over by this big paper I'm writing for history," she said. "How about you?"

Richard hung his head and acted like he was upset. He took her hand and led her to a quiet corner to talk. He went into great detail about how lonely he was and how much he wanted to start a new life.

"I came to meet a girl that I used to know, but like everything else in my life, it was a bust. She promised to meet me but didn't show up." He looked like he hadn't slept in days.

"I'm sorry," she said. "I wish there was something I could do to help." Jenny forgot about her history paper and focused on Richard. She put her hand on his shoulder and asked him what he wanted to do.

"I've got to switch things up," he confided. "I've got to move, but I can't get a job that pays enough to cover rent. Ya know what I really want to do?"

Jenny listened. "What's that?"

"I haven't told anyone this because no one would believe me. But I feel I can tell you. I want to travel. More than anything, I want to see

Europe. But I can't make plans if I can't make money."

"Well, my friend," Jenny said with a grin, "This is one problem I can fix. My father is always looking for help.

It's landscaping, so it pays well, and if I ask him, I'm certain he'll start you right away. One solution at a time." She laughed. "Let's move on to issue number two."

"I need someone to talk to, someone who will believe in me and trust me. I shared my secret with you. You're easy to talk to, and I feel like I'm not so alone in the world." He shook his head. "I'm tired of being lonely."

Jenny was surprised. "You can always come find me when you need me. I'll be here for you. For now, though, I'll talk to my dad about you when I go home this weekend."

She gave him a friendly hug and told him to cheer up.

She left him with a smile and a wave.

He watched her walk away, almost gloating to himself. He figured he had her eating out of his hand. That night at home, Richard gathered Moss and Samantha to tell them about his meeting with

Jenny. As he helped Samantha with her needle, he shared a story. It was about a girl from high school a few years ago. "Her name was Samantha, too," he said.

Samantha listened more closely, suddenly interested to hear what Richard's Samantha had done to make Richard so interested in their plan.

"I'd wait for her after school and walk her home. At first she was polite to me, kinda shy. We talked about movies. We both liked them. We'd quote lines back and forth. Then one day, I got up to her front door. I knew her parents weren't home, and I asked to come in. She said no."

Richard breathed heavily as he relived the moment. "I waited, and when she opened her door, I pushed my way in and started kissing her. She struggled, but I was stronger and pushed her toward the couch. I got on top of her and she bit my cheek. She screamed, and this big ass dog comes from the kitchen, barking and scaring the hell out of me. I got off and ran to the door. I yelled at her that she couldn't play me like that and not put out. She yelled something to the dog, and I left."

Richard shook his head. "All this women's rights stuff. They think they can say no whenever they want. Well, I got news for them."

Moss agreed with Richard. Samantha wasn't so sure. Even so, the idea for Richard to work for Jenny's father played right into their hands. Their plan to ruin Jenny was taking shape.

Moss chimed in, "If her father owns the company, I'll bet you can get money from them, too."

Richard agreed. "I already thought about that. I can check out what equipment or stuff we can steal; the turnover for that shit is amazing."

The trio, sitting cross-legged on Moss's bathroom floor, crunched numbers and made deadlines.

"We're so close to the final piece," Moss said to Richard, who laughed maniacally.

"If I can get her to marry me, the possibilities are endless. You should've seen the look on her face when I said I wanted to go to Europe." Richard snuffed out his half-smoked cigarette and slipped out of the room.

Samantha curled up against Moss's flannel covered chest. "That bitch is going to beg for mercy. So much for *Little   Miss   Perfect.*"

Jenny convinced her father to hire Richard. Richard talked fast to convince him that he was a great guy and a dedicated worker. However, Jack wasn't as easy to convince. He knew all about Richard. His reputation as a thief and a liar was all over town. His family and friends were heavy into drugs, and he had even done time at one point for selling it.

Jack tried to keep his dad from hiring him, but his dad's mind was made up. It was what Jenny wanted so that was the way of it.

Those first weeks, father and son both kept an eye on him, so he wasn't able to steal anything. This only made Richard want more, so he turned up the heat on pursuing Jenny.

By now, Jenny was busier than ever. Midterms were coming up, so she didn't have much free time to see Michael. She often thought of their time together in the house. She longed to go back to him. But then she would wonder if he was right for her, or if she was right for him.

In the middle of midterm exams, Richard surprised her with a visit. She took him to a cafeteria near campus for lunch, and they spent the afternoon catching up. Richard was very grateful that Jenny had gotten him the job. He went on and on about how much he enjoyed working with his hands. He complimented her on her hard work and how well she was doing—something Michael didn't seem to care about.

She was explaining the classes she would be able to transfer to if she made it to Italy when he interrupted her.

"What would you think if I told you that I want to travel sooner than I thought?" Richard looked for her reaction. "I saved some money, and I think it's enough for a one-way ticket."

Jenny was surprised to see the transformation in Richard. Instead of the lonely, needy guy she remembered, he sounded excited about the possibilities in his life. "Are you talking about moving to Europe now? There's a lot more to it than buying a ticket, you dork. You have to have a job lined up, a place to stay, and food. You don't just fly to Europe and hope for the best."

Richard took her hand. "You see, I don't know what to do by myself. I just want to get out of here. If you come with me, we could figure it all out together. You know how I feel about you. We obviously want the same things, and you're so smart. You can help me get settled. You and I can do anything if we do it together."

Jenny was shocked by what he said. He knew that the idea of traveling was her vulnerability. She wanted it more than anything. The difference was that she was willing to wait until the time was right, and she had all the details.

He just wanted to cut and run.

Jenny went back to campus and stayed in her room thinking about all the crazy ideas she and Richard had talked about.

She warmed up to the idea of running away and started thinking about it seriously. Why not? She didn't care about how little she felt for Richard or how he felt for her, but the idea of traveling excited her. It was so much simpler than with Michael. She didn't want to upset Michael, but seriously, the way he captured her thoughts completely was just too much too fast.

After she finished her midterm exams, she went back to her parents' house for the break and planned to meet Michael. He'd invited her to go out with him for an early supper.

As they were leaving the restaurant, he ran into one of his friends, and they were talking business. Jenny walked to the shop next door instead of waiting for him. She looked around at the clothes and browsed through a rack of cashmere sweaters. A male sales associate surprised her and asked if she needed some help.

She smiled sweetly and joked about how she wasn't used to seeing attractive men sell clothing to women.

He introduced himself as Joshua. "My aunt owns the shop, so I help her out sometimes. Can I show you this collection that just came in?"

She followed him to the back of the store. He held a cashmere sweater close to her, so she could feel the softness. "It's almost like pashmina. This would look great on you."

She declined. "I'm really not interested, thank you. Just looking." They made small talk, and Jenny made him laugh with her facial expressions of distaste at some of the outfits he showed her.

At that moment, Michael came in. All he heard was Jenny giggling as she played along after Joshua pulled yet another ugly outfit off the rack. "You're out of your mind," she yelled. "What do I look like?"

That was all Michael needed to hear. He stormed to the back of the store, grabbed Joshua, spun him around, and punched him dead in the face. Blood gushed from his nose, and he fell backward into the dress rack.

Jenny screamed at Michael to knock it off, pushed him outside, and climbed into the car with Michael at the wheel.

Michael drove like an old lady on sedatives back to his house. Still, Jenny was so scared she didn't say a word all the way back. Michael kept looking over at her and huffing. Once inside, he threw his keys down and turned to her.

"What the hell is wrong with you? You do not go wandering off without me."

"Are you kidding me? You just scared the crap out of me. You were completely out of control," she yelled back.

"What do you mean I scared you?" he said. "I was protecting you. That guy was all over you. God only knows what he would've done if I hadn't shown up."

Jenny's fists tightened. "I cannot handle your anger. It's not the first time you've lost it over some meaningless comment. This is insane. I am perfectly capable of defending myself. We were playing around, and you really hurt him."

Michael's voice lowered. "Yeah well, I don't care. He got what he deserved."

Jenny muttered, "I hope you never feel you need to teach me a lesson. You going to kick my ass, too?"

"Seriously? You think I would do something like that to you?"

"I'm not sure right now. Maybe you need a little anger management."

"You sound like my father." Michael sounded offended. He walked closer to her, and it looked like he was working to contain his ill temper. "Is that what they teach you in your beloved psych class? Diagnose the man who loves you and tell him what treatment he needs?"

Jenny resented his mocking tone, so she curled up on the couch and sat speechless.

Michael poured himself some whiskey and sat across from her "So, what...you're not talking to me now?" Michael swirled the drink in his glass.

"I'm done talking. I told you what I think, and you don't care, so what's the point? I told you that your temper and your random violence scare me. If my fear isn't enough for you to control it, then I don't have anything else to say."

"Violence. You call that violence? Defending you is violence?"

"Don't yell at me."

Michael threw his drink on the floor, and glass shards scattered everywhere. His eyes were like fire, and he flipped the table on its side. The crash echoed in the room as he stormed out.

Jenny began to cry.

After a few moments, Michael returned and slowly wrapped his arms around her. He wiped away her tears, and whispered, "I'm sorry. I don't know why that happened. I want to protect you, but I don't want you to be scared. I love you."

Jenny gathered her purse and sweater and asked Michael to take her back to campus. He tried to convince her to stay with him, but that wasn't going to happen.

They rode back in silence, and when he pulled up in front of her dorm, she wasted no time getting out of the car. No goodnight kiss, no words. She barely waited for the car to park before she jumped out and walked up the steps.

Michael pounded on the steering wheel and sped off squealing his tires.

Jenny didn't speak to Michael for a few weeks. When she didn't return his calls, Michael knew she was still mad and figured he'd better give her some time to cool off. But her words chafed, and his impatience consumed him.

Oliver's house was still Jenny's safe place. There was no drama. They had resumed their friendship and Oliver hadn't spoken of love again. His family were genuinely kind people. They loved Jenny and had always made her feel welcome.

One day, she flopped down on her belly and bumped Oliver while he fiddled with the strings on his guitar. He playfully scolded her, "Watch it, freak."

"Sorry," Jenny replied. "Being here is a huge relief from campus. I have so much crap to deal with, it's great to just hang out and de-stress."

Jenny sat up on her elbows. "I need your honest opinion about something. What do you think is better? A guy who has everything like money, power, and whatever. He loves this woman and wants to marry her, but they have nothing in common. The other guy loves the same woman, but he is not rich and powerful. He, on the other hand, has tons in common with her."

Oliver felt a sudden rush. He had to remind himself that these guys she talked about were not him. He cleared his throat and talked about his parents' marriage. They talked to Oliver about how important common goals and dreams were. He told her that working hard together is half the fun in a relationship. "Accomplishing things together and riding out the storms together. That's a real relationship," he said, putting his hand on his heart.

He was being honest and sincere about these convictions, but Jenny could detect a flicker of hope in her dear friend. Jenny gave him a hug and thanked him for his advice. "You're so smart," she said. "I knew I could count on you."

Oliver was happy to help, but felt confused. He wouldn't reveal it in words, but the guitar chords he played were plucked with his tension.

On the other side of town, Richard was still plotting. He knew just how to play his role with Jenny. He knew enough about what she liked and what she wanted. When he spoke, he was always calm and never lost his temper. The last day of her freshman year, Richard arranged a dinner date with Jenny to celebrate. He made arrangements with the waiter to surprise her. As their very elegant meal was ending and they waited for dessert to be served, the waiter brought two crystal glasses and poured champagne.

A second waiter brought a tray with two beautiful tiramisu desserts. The plates were the same, except hers had red candies arranged in the shape of a heart. She smiled at him and his sweet gestures. Then, Richard stood and moved to her side of the table. Diners at nearby tables watched as he dropped to one knee and presented an open velvet box with a radiant diamond ring inside. "Oh my God," she squealed. "What is this?"

"You have been so good to me," he began. "You have touched my heart like nobody has, and I can't imagine one day of my life without you. Please make me the happiest guy alive? Marry me?"

Jenny didn't respond. Her head was spinning between Michael's ring and his awful temper. Oliver's advice about riding out storms together came to her. And here was Richard, this guy who really got her. She helped him to his feet and motioned him back to his chair. She inhaled a big gulp of the now warm champagne.

Richard asked quietly, "Don't you want me?" His eyes searched hers. Everybody in the restaurant stared at them, waiting for Jenny's answer.

Jenny assured him it wasn't him. She squeezed his hand and tried to make him understand that she must finish school. She had things she needed to figure out. It was so soon, and what about her family? She hadn't even discussed him with them, yet. They would freak out if she ran off and married someone without their approval. He wasn't even going to ask her father? She loved her father and couldn't just spring this on him. There were rules.

While she still rambled, Richard grabbed her hand and slid the ring on—right below the one Michael had given her. Jenny's heart fluttered inside her chest. Did he notice? Would she have to reveal her agonizing affair with Michael?

Richard did notice, but he didn't care. Marriage wasn't the end goal for him, anyway. "You are everything to me, Jenny. I can't wait to make all of our dreams come true. Together."

Jenny smiled and finished her champagne.

She spent the next few days pondering her situation.

She went to her parents' for brunch on Sunday and tried to think of the best way to break the news. She told them she knew it was soon, but Richard's kindness and desire for travel were just a couple of the reasons why she was seriously considering accepting his proposal. They were not happy, but at least they listened.

In the middle of their conversation, Jack walked into the house and overheard just enough. He barged through the kitchen door.

"Are you fucking out of your mind?" he screamed. "Do you even know this asshole? He's a criminal. He runs drugs with gangs. He's messing with your head."

"What do you know?" she screamed back at him. "He's good to me. We want the same things, and he's not who you think he is. He loves me."

"Wow, he's really brainwashed you." Jack slammed his car keys on the countertop. "You honestly believe his bullshit. I thought you were smarter than that."

"Jack, Jenny—" Their father rose from his chair, but they were beyond listening.

Jenny stood and yelled, "Shut up, and butt the hell out. I don't need your fucking approval."

Jack slapped her across the face. In an instant, she fell to the ground with wide eyes, shocked that her brother had physically harmed her.

He reached for her shirt, grabbing it, and pulling her up from the ground.

"It's your life, Jenny. Do what you want. But if you marry this asshole and things go south, don't come here looking for help because you won't get it from me," he said through gritted teeth.

Jack let go of her shirt, and she grabbed her purse and ran out the door. Her cheek stung, and it made Jenny more determined than ever to marry Richard. She wanted away from all these men in her life that had tempers like little boys.

She knew she had to tell Michael, but was not looking forward to his reaction.

After much thought, she showed up at Michael's house. She stood before the tall woodpaneled door and rang the bell. Michael was glad to see her, but quickly noticed the bruise on her cheek. He rushed her inside and turned her to look at her face.

"What happened? Who did this?" he asked.

"It doesn't matter. I need to talk to you," she answered. "What the hell, Jenny? It matters to me; I'll kill the bastard. Who hit you?"

"It was Jack," she said quietly. "We got into an argument, and he lost it. It's no big deal. He was mad."

"What could have made him that mad? I'll ask him myself," he said scrambling for his phone.

Jenny begged him not to. She convinced him that it was over, and that what she needed was for him to stay with her and make her feel better. She tried to convince him that they needed a serious talk.

Michael conceded and held her until she calmed down.

She dropped into his arms, and he carried her to bed where she fell into an exhausted sleep.

The next day, before Jenny woke up, Michael was determined to find out what happened.

He found Jack in his office, working on his computer.

Jack welcomed Michael with his usual greeting. "Dude, come on in."

"Sorry to bug you at work." Michael offered a handshake.

"No, it's all right. Any time man," Jack said.

Michael got quiet. "I wanted to talk to you about Jenny."

"Did she call you?" Jack looked concerned.

"No, she came to my house." Michael's voice was sharp. "Her face is all jacked up. She said you hit her. What the hell happened?"

Jack looked shocked. "She went to your house? Seriously, has she lost her mind? Yeah, I slapped her. She's out of control. She's making me nuts."

"What the hell did she do? Where do you get off hitting her? She won't tell me anything."

Jack stood. "Oh, so she didn't tell you she's planning to marry that dirt bag Richard? She gets him a job, falls for his bullshit, and now she's going to marry him and run off. I don't think so.

So yeah, I slapped her. Maybe it knocked some sense into her."

Michael was speechless. He paced to the window and back. His collar felt hot, so he loosened his tie and looked at Jack for answers.

Jack told Michael that his sister had been tricked by Richard into believing that he was a great guy and not the prick that everyone in town knew him to be. He explained that when Jenny revealed her involvement with Richard, he lost his temper.

Michael was furious. He told Jack that he felt like killing Richard, but first he had to find him.

Even though Jack understood where Michael was coming from, he convinced Michael not to do anything stupid. "I know what you mean. Let's think this thing through."

Jenny was sitting at the dining table. When Michael returned, she stood to greet him. His usual tender glance was gone, and a glare took its place. He walked toward her and pulled off his tie. "What's wrong?" She felt unsafe.

"You were gone a while." She waited for an answer.

Michael stared at her for a long time. She could tell he was working hard to be calm. "What have I done to you?" he asked.

Jenny acted as though she had no idea what Michael was talking about. This made him furious. He turned around and flipped the table to the floor. He threw the chairs one at a time and screamed at her that Jack had told him everything.

Jenny was crying and frightened, walking backward till she got to the stairs and tripped. She sat and her hand flew to her face. Michael walked over to her and grabbed her hand to make her stand up and face him.

He screamed, "You want to marry someone else, huh? You want to marry that piece of shit, Richard? What the fuck are you doing? What the fuck are you thinking?

What am I? Am I just a game to you? You dump me whenever you want and pick me up whenever you need?"

Michael let her go, and she fell back to the step crying.

He got quiet and begged her for a response. "Why him? You've been cheating this whole time."

She rushed to him and tried to explain. "I never cheated. You're the only one I was with. He and I have been friends for a while, and it has just changed. It's different now. We want the same things, and I'm tired of working so hard and getting nowhere. I want to go away with him and really live my life." She couldn't tell if he heard her words or if he was too consumed with anger.

"What I want doesn't fit into your life here," she said. "We're at different places right now. I'm sorry...I need to take this shot. I know nobody likes him, but he is so good to me."

"He's good to you?" Michael faced her again. "I wasn't good enough to you?" Michael threw a vase from the foyer table, and the echo of shattering glass heightened their tension.

"Well, let's just fucking burn down this palace. Go off and satisfy yourself because it's all about you. Is that what you want?"

Frightened of his temper, Jenny shook her head no.

He moved swiftly across the living room. "I know what to do with you. You think you want to dump me? You think he is better than me?" He scooped her up and carried her to his bedroom. He dropped her onto the bed where they had made love before, but this time it was different.

He held both her hands in one of his as he reached up her skirt, pulling off her underwear.

She tried to talk, but he silenced her voice with his mouth on hers. His kiss was hot and wet and his strength was overbearing. Before she knew it, they were tangled in passionate lovemaking, and she remembered how lost in excitement she felt.

She was still scared, but fear and anger were replaced with his body on hers, a feeling of calm and safety. She felt herself giving in to his strength, and as they moved together, he became more and more forceful. Afterword, she lay in his arms.

Michael rested on one elbow. "You have no idea what you're giving up. Nobody will ever love you like I do."

Jenny knew that was true. She lay with him in bliss, like nothing had changed. Only, everything had changed.

Daylight came slow, a welcome contrast to the passionate fury of the night before. Jenny could see Michael through the crack in the balcony doorway. She draped a bed sheet over her bare body and surprised him. He nearly spilled the coffee he was drinking when he saw her in the morning glow.

"You know I have to leave soon," Jenny told him. "I shouldn't have come here in the first place."

"No matter how far away you go and how hard you try to escape, we are meant to be together. You'll come back to me," Michael said. "I just know it."

Jenny was crying. She hated letting him down, denying him his fantasies.

"I won't come back," she said. "I can't."

"We've made love a lot, Jenny. You don't think it's possible I could have gotten you pregnant?"

"Michael, why would you say such a thing? Threats aren't the best foundation for a relationship."

"I'll do whatever it takes to win you over for good," Michael said. "If I have to ruin your idiotic marriage, then so be it."

Jenny couldn't contain her tears. He was upsetting her. "You can't keep living this double life, dreaming of far off places with Richard and sleeping in my bed. It'll catch up to you," Michael warned.

But Jenny was done with the conversation.

"I'm going back to campus. I don't have to stay and listen to this," Jenny said. "We would never work. I am not good for you, and one day, you'll realize that."

Michael called her a taxi, and as it sped off with Jenny inside, he didn't bother to watch her go.

Jenny had a rough time during the end of the semester.

She was confused. This was so crazy. She planned everything. She was supposed to be studying for finals, but her hours at the library were filled with worry about Michael, worry that she could be pregnant. Maybe Oliver had been right. She hadn't planned this.

Lying on Oliver's bed one afternoon, Jenny vented her frustrations. He always had a way of calming her nerves with sage advice. When Oliver was a few minutes into a deep thought, his mom knocked rapidly on his door.

"May I come in? It's urgent," she said.

"Sure," Oliver replied, unlocking and opening the door to his mother standing pale-faced and wide-eyed.

She handed a copy of *The Oakland Press* to Oliver. It was flipped to the Obituaries section.

"Samantha O. Bryant, age 22, died on Wednesday, August 5..."

Oliver's jaw dropped, and he passed the newspaper to Jenny.

Samantha had always been more of an acquaintance than a friend to Jenny. But still, this news hurt. Rumor had it that she'd died of a drug overdose. Jenny believed it. It was true. Moss had never been good for her. This is the only way it could have ended.

Jenny sighed, a tear rolled down her cheek, and she and Oliver hugged for what seemed like hours.

Richard and Moss hovered around Samantha's grave.

Moss was distraught. He couldn't believe he had lost another girlfriend to this. It wouldn't stop him, though. Or Richard.

"We have to finish this out," Moss said. "For Samantha. She would have wanted nothing more than to take Jenny down. We're doing this for her."

Richard nodded his head in agreement, and the two turned away from the grave and headed home.

During the summer break, Jenny moved off campus and into a house Richard had rented. She was thrilled that Richard agreed to stay until she graduated, and it gave her time to plan their travel in Europe. Her family was furious, and she was careful to avoid her brother.

They chose their wedding date, but since everyone disagreed with her decision, there was really nobody to invite. Not even her friend Sarah supported her. She didn't care much for Richard, but she loved Jenny and wanted her to be happy. The day was approaching, and Jenny was distraught. She was late. She was so afraid she was pregnant that she was making herself sick. Or was she sick because she was pregnant? Her head was spinning.

Jack and Michael had a business meeting that was tense and awkward. Neither of them had seen Jenny for a while, and they were careful not to speak of her.

But Jack was willing to try anything and wondered if Michael might be the only one who could convince her. When Michael was about to leave, Jack asked, "So, have you heard?"

"Heard what?" Michael turned back.

"My moron sister is marrying the prick tomorrow at City Hall." Jack frowned. "Go see her. Try again. She won't talk to me. You're really my only hope."

Michael sighed heavily. "I tried. There's no getting through to her. Besides, I don't even know where she lives now." Jack pulled a folded piece of paper out of his shirt pocket and handed it to him.

"Thank you, Sarah." He grinned.

Michael smacked Jack on the back, and he rushed away. "I owe you one," he shouted behind him.

When Michael found her place, he rang the bell and moved out of sight. She opened the door, walked out to see who was there, and he stepped in front of her.

"What the hell?" she snapped. "What are you are doing here?"

"I came to take you with me. This is not happening." He picked her up and carried her to his car.

"Michael," Jenny yelled. "What are you talking about?" "You are not marrying him." He spoke slowly as if he were giving directions to a small child. He locked the doors and peeled away from the curb.

Jenny was mad and scared. When they got to his house, he pulled her in and carried her to the bedroom. He locked the door, caressed her, and slipped off her clothes. She told him to stop, but he was moving too fast. Jenny protested, "You can't do this. I'm getting married tomorrow."

"Not if I can help it." His voice changed. He sounded as if he were the one marrying Jenny tomorrow. "We are meant to be together, Jenny. You know it's true."

Michael stroked her body. He pushed himself inside her, making her gasp. He kissed her hard, keeping her from screaming. She tried to resist him, but she eventually surrendered under his weight. She thought of the way he loved her so completely. How could she resist the way he made her feel? The forcefulness and passion, then the tenderness. The gentle feel of his hands. This man overwhelmed her, and she was astonished by the way she felt all over again. She could not imagine anything else being like this.

As they lay on the bed, Jenny looked at his handsome face and whispered, "Why? Why do you do this to me?"

Michael smoothed her hair. "I told you, I love you. You are mine. You are all that I need to be happy. You love me. You still have my ring, and for all we know, you're carrying my baby. I am certain that our love will last. This is our house, and I'll be waiting with open arms."

Jenny looked away. "I'm not changing my mind," she said in a quiet voice. "Life short, and I want to experience adventure. I think Richard is my adventure."

Michael looked as if he had just died. He called a taxi to take her back home. She should have felt so angry with Michael, so violated. Instead she felt torn in two directions on her tearful ride back to Richard.

Jenny began her wedding day at the salon around the corner. She and Richard said their I-do's in front of the judge, and Jenny welled up with tears when he pronounced them husband and wife. She felt sick. Had she just taken vows to love a man that she really didn't know?

Visions of Michael floated in her mind. The more she scolded herself not to think of him, the more his face became etched in her thoughts. His face, beside her as they lay in bed the day before.

Later at home, Richard found her at their desk, staring out the window.

"We should be in bed, baby." He pawed at the front of her dress.

She looked at him and quickly turned her head, "I'm really not feeling well. I need to be alone for a while."

Richard went to the bedroom, alone, and she put her head on the desk and cried.

That night of the wedding, Michael had gone out and gotten drunk. His friends took his keys and dropped him at his mother's house. When she asked him what was bothering him, he broke down in her arms and cried like a child. He explained what Jenny had done and how brokenhearted he was.

"She's married now, Mom. My goddess is gone forever. What am I going to do?"

As much as she tried to comfort him, he was inconsolable. His mom held his head. "Michael, if it was meant to be, she will return to you."

The next day after work, Richard came home to find Jenny napping. He quietly took his clothes off and slid into bed with her. He touched her gently and moved on top of her, kissing her neck. She startled awake and pushed him away. "Wait," she shouted.

Richard moved closer again. "I've waited long enough."

She tried to slow him down and make him understand that she really wasn't ready for that, but he didn't care. His attitude was that she was his wife now, and she had no choice but to have sex with him whenever he chose. His landscape work had made him much stronger, and she couldn't get her tiny body out from under his weight. She was disgusted with herself. He was licking her cheeks and neck and running his tongue all over her face and breasts.

Richard could tell that Jenny wasn't interested. He knew she really had no desire to have sex with him. The thought of making her squirm delighted him. She lay still with her head turned away from his hot breath and closed her eyes tight.

"Jenny baby, open your eyes," he whispered.

She looked at him, and he gave her an evil grin. "I'm good at this, you'll see."

"Just stop licking me for God's sake; I don't like it." She closed her eyes again.

Richard licked her eyelids, and she yelled. "I told you I don't like that."

He laughed hard and loud. Ignoring her protests, he slowly started down her body. She clamped her legs shut and refused to let him get closer, but he overpowered her, and she could feel the stubble on his rough face scraping against her. This guy disgusted her to the point of being ill. He tried again to kiss her mouth. "Really?" She thought to herself. "You force oral sex and then want to kiss me? Freaking animal!"

He forced himself inside her. Rough, despite her tears.

When she didn't respond the way he wanted her to, he became enraged and really started hurting her. Michael had never hurt her.

Her mind was frantic knowing that this was the future she had chosen. This was the polar opposite of lovemaking.

How could she endure sex with this barbarian for the rest of her life? When he'd finished, she turned away from him, closed her eyes, and whispered, "What have I done?"

As weeks went by, Michael's mother was worried that he still lived alone in the house he'd built for Jenny. She didn't share his hope for a miracle. She often dropped in on him with the excuse of bringing him meals. She'd tried to introduce him to her friend's daughter to distract him from his loneliness and maybe help him move on, but he would have no part of it.

"But Michael," she said, "Christa is a lovely girl. She's looking for someone to settle down and have a family with." Michael just smiled and ignored her.

A few months later, Jenny was still feeling ill, and the worry and wait for her period were impossible to endure. By now, her belly was a melon. In her mind, there was no way she wasn't pregnant. She made a doctor's appointment and wondered if she should tell her family. She picked up the phone, but the thought of her brother crowing that he was right about Richard made her stop.

Besides, she didn't want her parents to worry about her being pregnant or suffering from Richard's wrath.

Somehow she would figure out how to deal with Richard herself.

She went to the doctor and the pregnancy test was negative. He ordered some tests, but she threw away the order on her way out the door. All that mattered was that she wasn't pregnant.

She dove back into her schoolwork and tried to forget about everything else. One afternoon when Jenny was tutoring, Sarah came to pick her up from school for a coffee break.

"I'm just finishing up," Jenny called to Sarah in the doorway. She turned back to the freshman student, who sat at the table covered in history research notes and his laptop. "Remember what we talked about. Organize your time, and work a little every day. Always go back to the professor's assignment. Keep looking for the *how* and *why* of your argument. Consider the context of the Harlem Renaissance writers in New York during their time, not our time."

"Yeah, it's easy when you say it, but then I go home, and it's all confusing again."

Jenny sighed. "That's just your mindset talking. This work is brain exercise. You work out your body for wrestling, right?" She watched the freshman nod. "Think of this paper as building mental muscle. The work is what's important, more important than the grade."

He thanked her and they set up a time for the following week. Sarah hadn't seen Jenny in her role as a tutor before, and she could see her enthusiasm. "You were really good with that guy," she said.

"I've been working with him on a few assignments. It's affirming when he brings me a paper we've worked on, and I see his grade. Now I'm more of a cheerleader. He's remembering more of the steps by himself."

They found a table in the coffee shop and ordered lattes. "So how are things with you and Oliver?" Jenny tried to sound casual.

Sarah looked at her friend. "Jenny…Jenny…you weren't going to tell me, were you?"

"What do you mean?"

"Oliver told me everything, including your loyalty to me and how you didn't want to ruin the friendship we shared. Now we're closer than ever. I think you tipped the scales in my favor."

"It's a relief. It's hard to keep secrets from you," Jenny said. "Oliver's a great guy, and he didn't want anything to come between you."

She considered telling Sarah about her Neanderthal husband, but knew she couldn't.

Sarah wasn't one to betray a confidence, but Richard was extreme. Could Sarah keep a secret like this? Jenny had made a horrible decision to marry, and only Jenny could fix it.

"So tell me about married life. Is it everything you thought? Are you making your plans for Europe?"

"We're very different people, and I think we're both adjusting." Jenny tried to be as truthful as possible. "We're both pretty busy with school and work. I haven't had time for any Europe plans, yet."

Jenny talked about her house. Sarah talked about an open mic night where Oliver tried out one of his new songs. They were excited to get his music out into the world.

On her way home, Jenny felt more relaxed than she had in weeks. For an hour, she forgot about Richard and her ill health.

When she got home, the mailbox lid was partly open, and an oversized manila envelope was stuffed inside. She dropped her book bag onto the porch and tore open the envelope from the bank. Richard had been secretly running up her credit cards and using her bank card to make weekly withdrawals from her accounts. He was her husband. If it kept him from bothering her, it might be worth the money. She threw the envelope away.

Jenny still wasn't herself, even a few weeks after her appointment. She was tired all the time and her stomach was so upset she could barely keep anything down. She went to the drug store to get some antacid.

They rang up her medicine and water bottle, but when she swiped her debit card, it was declined. "There must be some mistake," she told the clerk. "This has never happened before." She brought out her wallet and paid with cash.

She took a taxi to the bank and asked the manager for an explanation. He pointed to his computer monitor. The list of transactions showed several large withdrawals over the past few months. The day after the direct deposit from her trust cleared, it was withdrawn. Richard had cleaned her out. How could she have been so foolish? The realization that everyone else was right jolted her again. Richard wasn't just taking small amounts; he'd stolen everything.

She went home and waited for him, the shock too painful to put into words. Soon he came in, grubby and dirty as usual, fully expecting her to leap to her feet to greet him like some dutiful little wife from the fifties.

He looked at her face and frowned. "Hello?" he barked.

Jenny wasted no time. "My debit card was declined today. The bank manager said you've been withdrawing money regularly. All my savings are gone. My trust fund money is gone. What the hell did you do with over a hundred thousand dollars?" She slammed her fist on the table. "And where the hell do you get off taking my money? My life savings. How could you do something like this?" She swung her arm in a wide arc.

A curl of loathing touched the corner of Richard's mouth. He started to lie and tell her he had moved the money to a joint account to save for their move, but decided it wasn't worth the effort. "The money's gone, goddess. Get over it."

"I want it back. I have tuition and bills to pay. What the fuck were you thinking?"

Richard's face was red. "Stop telling me what you want. I don't give a shit what you want. I never have."

Jenny shook her head. "I should have listened to Jack.

He said you were nothing more than a hood rat thief. I should've listened."

Richard moved quickly. He grabbed her hair and jerked her to him, forced her to kiss him. But she turned her head away. He knocked her down and slapped her face repeatedly, until her mouth bled and her eye swelled.

She fumbled around and found her purse on the end table. She pulled out her bank card and tossed it at him.

"Here," she said." Go have a ball, get high, do whatever it is you do. That's all you ever wanted."

Richard laughed. "Damn straight that's all I ever wanted. Look at you. Who could want you?" He snatched the card from her, bent down, and twisted her arm behind her back until it hurt. In her ear, he whispered, "Just wait," and he bit her earlobe hard.

He straightened up, put the bank card in his wallet, and put his wallet in his back pocket. He reached down and grabbed her by the wrist, dragged her to the door, and pushed her down the basement stairs and to the center of the room, by the structural beam. "I'm ready for you, goddess." She lay crying on the floor, and he stood over her unbuckling his belt. He pulled at her legs and lifted her skirt. She screamed, and he slapped her mouth again. He raised her up pinning her against the washing machine and rammed himself into her. She couldn't breathe from the pain. She thought she would split in half. He humped her like a dog until he exploded inside her. He dropped her to the floor and zipped up his ragged jeans.

She curled up in a heap, crying, only lifting her head as he started up the stairs. "You're a fucking animal! You just wait," she threatened.

He stormed over and kicked her in the back. Pain shot through her trembling frame.

"Stay here like an animal. That's all you are. You're a stupid animal that fell into a trap. Your money is the only thing I ever wanted, and now I have it. You were so easy. Moss and Samantha were right. You were so certain that every man in the world couldn't possibly resist you.

You're so beautiful. Everyone loves you; everyone wants you, blah, blah, blah.

"Well nobody wants you now, do they? You're nothing. You're broke, you're used goods, and honey, you just ain't that great a lay to stick around and put up with your shit."

He crossed the basement and opened a trunk in the corner. He pulled out a couple of blankets, a rope, a loaf of white bread, a gallon bottle of water, and a bucket.

He made his way to Jenny, who had backed into a corner to get as far from him as possible. He dug his fingers into the crown of her head and yanked her up in the air so she was hanging there by her hair. He hauled her back toward the center of the room, to the beam, with a fat iron eye latch screwed in. Richard looped the rope through the latch and tied Jenny's right wrist to the post, giving her just enough slack so she could get to the blankets on the floor—and the bucket. He put the bread and water where she could see them, but just out of her reach.

"Welcome, home, goddess," he said. "I always wanted me a mutt named Goddess."

She couldn't believe how bad things had gotten. What was his plan? Didn't he realize that, sooner or later, someone would wonder where she'd gone? She thought of her family and Michael. She tried to move her wrists, but they were tied to the beam and any movement made her skin burn. Watching Richard, her warden, sit across from her on the basement floor looking at his phone, she could only imagine what it was he stared at so intently.

"What have I done to you?" she asked him quietly.

"I just like to see you suffer, that's all," he answered.

"You really are sick. Everything I heard about you was true."

"I fooled you, didn't I?"

"You're a fucking liar, and you didn't fool anyone," she screamed.

He stood again, strode over to her like John Wayne, and kicked her in the ribs. "How's them ribs? Feel better now? Would you like to mouth off some more?"

"I don't feel anything anymore," she said. "Do whatever you want."

Richard stripped his clothes off quickly. He went to her, still tied to the beam, and forced himself on her again. She didn't fight. He grabbed and pinched her breasts hard, tried to make her scream.

Jenny laughed at him. "See. I feel nothing." She had figured out that if she took her mind away to Michael, and Richard touched her body, she could ignore whatever he did to her. This infuriated him.

Richard left and returned with a lighter and a knife. He leaned close and whispered in her ear.

"Now, do you want to see what this is for, or do I get a blow job?" He got off on the terror in her eyes.

"You're disgusting." She closed her eyes. "I told you, I don't feel anything. You want to kill me, go ahead, I don't care. I'm already dead."

"I will hear you scream and beg for mercy," he said. Richard held the lighter to the knife. When the color began to change, he put the knife close to her face, eyes, lips, and neck. She held her breath at the closeness of the heat from the metal. Finally, he pressed it hard against her lower back. A searing, sharp pain made her gasp and pass out. When she woke up, she saw the back of him walking away.

He crossed the basement again, climbed the steps two at a time and slammed the door. Within a minute or two, Jenny heard some banging and drilling, intermittent cussing, and finally the clunk of a big lock. "Ha. Enjoy that."

Jenny tried to get up, but she was too weak to move.

Her mouth and nose were bleeding, and her shoulder throbbed. Shivering on the floor, she listened. The bike roared down the driveway, and she knew he was gone. Alone with the pain, at least she was safe for now. But for how long? He would come back.

Oliver had noticed that Jenny wasn't in school for a few days. When she didn't return after a week, he was terrified. Terrified of what Richard might have done to her. He got into his van and drove over to their little house—where he'd never been invited to enter—but he'd cruised by at least once a week to see if everything looked okay.

When nobody answered the doorbell or phone, and he could see no movement, it took him less than five minutes to break in. Less than a minute to discover the industrial- size clasp and padlock on the basement door.

"Jenny," he yelled. "Jenny, are you down there?" He listened, and he thought he heard something thump, but it wasn't very loud.

It took longer to break into the garage and find something he could use to get through that basement door, but he finally did it and came away with a rusty ax. He'd have thought the whole neighborhood would be on his back, the racket he made chopping his way through that door, but nobody came, and there was no sound from the basement. He was so afraid that he thought he was going to puke.

Finally he cut the lock free and the door swung out of his way. He bolted down the stairs. Squinted in the dim light. It smelled like old urine and death. Then he saw her. Wrapped in an old, wool blanket.

"Oh, Jenny."

She was unconscious, but breathing. He untied her, cradled what was left of her in his arms, and carried her upstairs. He laid her on the couch and ran to the linen closet, where he found a hand towel and a sheet. He wet the hand towel and wrung it out, took both back to the couch, and wrapped Jenny in the clean sheet. He put the edge of the towel between her cracked lips. "Try to suck on this, Jen. You can do this. You can do anything you put your mind to."

Seventeen minutes later, Jenny was on a gurney in the ER at Troy Beaumont. A flurry of people in scrubs swarmed her and pushed Oliver toward the information lady. He knew she wanted him to fill out paperwork and probably come up with some insurance, but he had a job to do first.

Oliver wasn't leaving anything alone. He took off to find Richard. He knew where to find him. He drove past that group of slugs every morning. Oliver's speech was prepared as he pulled his van into the lot. Richard was perched on his bike with all his lowlife friends surrounding him.

Oliver walked toward them, practicing his line in his head, but when Richard stood, there were no words. He grabbed Richard by the shirt and threw him to the ground. A punch to the face, and then another, drew blood. Then the others stepped in. They pulled him off Richard and held his arms behind his back.

Richard got up and wiped the blood from his mouth.

He aimed all of his angry strength at Oliver's gut. He punched Oliver harder while the others held on.

Once Oliver caught his breath, he said, "Can't fight like a man, fucker?" He struck with words, his only remaining weapon. "You can't take me one on one? You need your little posse to keep me from fighting back. Did you need help while you beat up your wife, too?"

Oliver struggled to release himself. Richard beat him over again, yelling between every strike. "I'm gonna kill you, mother fucker. You should mind your own damn business."

Oliver managed to kick his foot up as hard as he could and knocked Richard in the balls. "That's for Jenny, asshole," he groaned.

Richard went down. After a few seconds, he dragged himself up from his knees and pulled a knife from his boot. He walked to Oliver, who was still held back but struggling. Richard stabbed him in the stomach, and the others let go. Oliver crumpled to the ground.

With a death grip on the knife, Richard reached up, grabbed Oliver's hair, and pulled his head back. Richard slit his throat without batting an eye. He walked off and lit a joint from his pocket. The others threw Oliver into the back of the van and drove off.

It was nearly a week later, after a frantic search by friends and loved ones, that the police came to tell Oliver's parents that they'd found Oliver's body in his van in the next town. The devastation was indescribable, and Oliver's distraught parents searched for answers.

Barely holding herself together, Sarah looked all over campus, but there was no sign of Jenny. Had she been with Oliver? Was she dead, too?

Two days passed before Jenny regained consciousness. She awoke in a private room overlooking a golf course, and she was still tied to the post. No. It was an IV in her arm. She tried not to think, but flits of memory of Richard and the rope and the knife and kicking—it was too much. She tossed the sheet back to assess the damage. Her feet were swollen, and her belly was still getting bigger.

A nurse came in—a strong-looking woman with kind eyes. She talked quietly and was matter of-fact about everything. She said a young man named Oliver had brought her in, and two days had passed.

The police had searched her house and called Social Services, who packed up a bag of things she might want. "Your brush and comb are in there, and a couple books from a shelf in the dining room are over there," she said, pointing to spots in her hospital room.

Jenny felt confused, but she wanted to get out of this place. "I'll take them. I have to go home."

The nurse put one finger on Jenny's hand and rubbed so lightly. "Let's not worry about that right now. You might never want to go back to that house."

Yes. That's right. "I never want to go back to that house." Jenny couldn't believe she was saying it aloud. It was like she was a robot. What if Richard found out—?

"Just take a sip of water for me and relax," the kind nurse said. "Dr. Scott is going to come in and talk with you this afternoon. Meanwhile, rest up. He wants you to get some sleep."

She winked, turned, and floated out the door.

At first, Jenny was unable to sleep. She kept wondering where Oliver was. If he had brought her in, it would be unlike him to just leave.

She'd been running through the worst possible-case scenarios when a young, handsome doctor came in. She guessed he'd brought along an extra-big dose of empathy, because he looked really serious. She knew she looked awful, but bruises and burns would heal.

He introduced himself and asked her where all the bruises and scars and rope burns came from. Jenny said she had been in a motorcycle accident. The doctor was a good listener, but said these were not the kinds of scars he'd seen from accident victims. Then, she saw something odd in his eyes. It was as if she could see him decide to set that problem aside. There must be something worse coming. She braced herself.

Dr. Scott took her hand and told her that test results confirmed that she had cancer. There were tumors on the uterus and the breast. He talked about treatments and today's hopeful outcomes, but Jenny could only hear the word *cancer*. This was why her belly looked like a volleyball. Jenny had seen cancer. She knew what it did.

The doctor reassured her. "We found this early. It can be treated. We remove the tumors and follow up with a little chemo, and there's no reason to believe we can't beat this."

His words were meant to comfort, but Jenny was terrified. "When?" she asked.

"As soon as possible."

Not the answer Jenny wanted to hear. The doctor tried again to calm her.

But Jenny sobbed. "I'm not crying because I'm afraid," Jenny said. "I'm crying because I lost my cousin to cancer. I watched her suffer through the chemo. It's terrible."

Dr. Scott talked to her about the advancements that had been made in the last few years. "There is new research every day. Some treatments now are so localized that they don't cause all of the side effects."

The doctor made sense. Maybe she could get through this. There was still hope.

Then, Dr. Scott decided to go back to the Richard problem. The doctor said she had been starved and dehydrated and was entirely too weak for the surgery right now, and he couldn't let her go home until she'd gained some weight and they got her hemoglobin up to at least ten.

The thought of going home and telling her family about what Richard had done crossed her mind dozens of times, but she thought there was no need to worry them or to put up with Jack saying, "I told you so."

Dr. Scott said, "The minute you're back to your healthy self, we'll do the first procedure, so you may as well hang out here."

She was going to argue, but there was a tone in his voice that told her that would be pointless. Besides, where would she go?

Chapter Three

Sarah broke the news to Jenny. Both of them visited Oliver's grave. The sky was overcast and the warblers and robins sang a soundtrack. Jenny liked to think they were performing for Oliver.

She kneeled on the ground and punched the soil above Oliver's lifeless body.

"Goodbye, my friend," she said solemnly.

She placed a single rose at the foot of the headstone and cried. Sarah pulled her away and back toward the car. Between her best friend's death, Richard's betrayal, her guilt over Michael, and now, her cancer diagnosis, Jenny had just about had enough. She felt like she was carrying the weight of the world on her frail shoulders.

The last Jenny heard, Richard had skipped out of town and to the border. She wouldn't have been surprised if he'd joined some sort of drug cartel. Although she felt secure, she couldn't stop herself from imagining his return. She slept with a knife sometimes, just to ease the jitters that seemed to come so frequently now.

The days before her surgery, Jenny spent alone.

Scared and unhappy, she didn't tell her mom, or anyone else about the horror she was going through. What about Michael? No, she couldn't dump this on him.

Sarah had been so hurt over Hanna, and Jenny had promised she'd never get sick. So Jenny ignored her calls and only sent short texts in reply to her many messages. She thought about her friend, Oliver. If there were anyone she'd want to help her through this surgery, it would be Oliver, with his amazing good spirits and good sense. But he's dead. That sent her into another bout of tears.

Between the tears, she began to get her affairs in order for the surgery. She notified the college and put her studies on hold. Her accounts were secure again, so Richard could not access them. Now all she had to do was figure out how she would take the next step—alone.

On surgery day, Dr. Emery and Dr. Scott greeted her. Emery was the surgeon who would remove the cancer, and Scott was the oncologist who would treat the disease afterward.

Dr. Scott thought how beautiful Jenny was and how unfortunate it was meeting her this way. She was the patient, and he, the doctor. Why couldn't they have met in a coffee shop over vanilla lattes and croissants? Nevertheless, he went about his medical duties.

Jenny was afraid of the IV, but Dr. Scott assured her he was an expert at this. He tied the band around her arm and slipped the needle in with hardly any pain at all. "See...told you." He smiled.

She knew he was flirting with her. She had seen that smile before. But she was too tired, too upset, to play along.

He spoke to her for a while as she waited to be taken down to surgery. Usually family members were with the patient, but Jenny was alone. She remained quiet.

Dr. Scott commented on her silence and she nodded. "Speaking takes energy. I'm using all my energy to keep calm and get through this operation. It's my own personal kind of meditation."

He smiled and patted her hand. "I'll leave you alone then. We'll meet up in recovery."

In the recovery room, Dr. Scott and a nurse were trying to wake Jenny up. She was slow to respond, but eventually she answered a few questions.

Later that evening, Dr. Scott stopped in to check on her and make sure she was comfortable. They talked about the successful surgery.

Jenny said, "This was a bit more serious than the appendectomy I had as a child. But surgery is surgery."

In the middle of the night, a nurse came to her side and found Jenny choking back tears. The nurse asked about the pain.

"I'm all right," she replied, fighting back tears and trying to sound normal.

She closed her eyes and pretended to fall asleep. Her mind was spinning, and all she could think about was how nice it would feel to have Michael's arms around her again. "He was right," she thought. "I do want to go back to him."

The nurse wasn't convinced by Jenny's act and wrote comments on her bed chart. The next morning, Dr. Scott popped his head into her room. "How's my quiet one today?"

She smiled and told him she was feeling better.

He asked her again about all the bruises and where could she go that she'd be safe. Jenny assured him that she lived alone and no one was abusing her. She understood Dr. Scott had to report her bruises, but what if her parents found out? Her father was proud of her independence and success in college. She couldn't tolerate the thought of her family feeling sorry for her for the cancer or for her choice in men.

Dr. Scott picked up on her expression and whispered, "Look, I understand you must be scared, but I know rope burns when I see them. The scars on your wrists tell a story. The other marks are typical of abuse. Have you reported any of this to the authorities?"

Jenny turned away and repeated, "There is no abuse. It was a motorcycle accident. I'm tired."

Three days later, Jenny was discharged. Dr. Scott set up her chemo for the end of the month and gave her a list of dos and don'ts during her recovery. As she was standing up from the wheelchair that had brought her down to the taxi, he took her hand and slipped her his cell phone number. "If you get into trouble or you need anything, anything at all, you call me. Day or night."

She thanked him, knowing full well what he meant, and the taxi sped away. For the next few weeks, she was careful to follow the doctor's orders to the letter. When she made sure to eat well and drink lots of water, her strength began to return and the feeling of illness was gone. The emotional pain lingered. She remembered Oliver playing his music in his backyard. If only Michael was here to help her, she wouldn't feel so lonely. He would have taken such good care of her.

Jenny moved to a small apartment. It was close to the hospital, and she was careful to leave no trail of where she'd gone. He would never find her again. Richard's house would not be her house any longer. The simplicity of the apartment appealed to her. It wasn't fancy or flashy. It was small and clean, and she had it all to herself.

Michael never thought about seeing anyone else. He held hope that someday Jenny would return to him, but he worried about her often and wished he knew how she was. He felt deep down that there was something wrong, but brushed it off as his own loneliness. He wanted to see her, but had no idea how to find her.

A couple more weeks went by, and Michael was still feeling that something was wrong. Jenny was somewhere, and she needed him. He was certain. He had dreamed about her not being well. He drove by her family house, knowing full well that she didn't live there anymore. What the hell, he thought, and he pulled in the drive. Jack was surprised and glad to see him.

"Have you heard anything from Jenny?" Michael asked "I went to campus and checked. Apparently, she hasn't been there since last semester. Sarah said that she heard Jenny was taking some online classes."

Michael frowned and touched his forehead. "Do you think they moved to Europe? Sarah should know something."

"No clue man. Jenny hasn't spoken to me since our fight."

Michael leaned against the porch railing. "I'm not sure.

I've had this nagging feeling for a while now. Like something's wrong. Maybe she's in trouble." His head was hurting, and he asked for a pain reliever.

Jack interrupted, "Me, too. Dude that's weird. I don't know what to do. Should we call the cops?

Maybe see if they could find her." He left for a glass of water and Tylenol.

Michael thought about it for a minute. When Jack returned, Michael said, "No, you know what, she knows where we are. If something were really wrong, she would've called one of us. Thanks, Jack." He gulped the pill and water. "Let me know if you hear from her."

Michael drove past the other house she had lived in and saw there was another family living there. It seemed they had been there for a while. He watched them for a moment and pounded the steering wheel in frustration. He sped away.

Jenny returned to Dr. Scott's care for her first round of chemo and battled the side effects of sickness. Dr. Scott was compassionate and checked on her regularly. The nurses had written again that she cried a lot, even in her sleep. When Dr. Scott confronted her on the third day of treatment, he expressed his concern that her emotional health might have a negative effect on her treatment.

Haunted with nightmares of Richard and the horrible things he had done to her; she nearly spilled the story. But she quickly changed her mind. "I'm done," she told him, the tension in her voice rising. "I don't want to be here anymore."

He gently explained that these treatments were a long process and that he understood her frustration.

She screamed at him. "You don't understand. I know what's coming. I'm not going to get better. Hell, I'm already dead!"

Dr. Scott tried to reassure her. "You have a very good chance of beating this, Jenny, and we'll help you every step of the way."

Jenny stood and spun around like a ballerina. Spinning outside of herself, spinning to escape Richard, and spinning to escape cancer. Any place was better than here, better than a hospital filled with pain. Michael had spun her around, making love to her. Now, it seemed so long ago.

Scott held her arms to slow her. "You're going to get dizzy. It's not good for you."

She took his hand to steady herself, and a hint of smile appeared through her tears. "You have no idea how much I needed that."

Jenny thought about calling Michael and her family. She tapped out the number and hung up quickly. Why make them unhappy? If she called Sarah, she knew she would run straight to Jenny's mom.

A few weeks later, in the shower, Jenny noticed her long hair was coming out in clumps. She was devastated. With a towel wrapped around her, she looked in the mirror. Tears trailed down her cheeks, but she grabbed the scissors from the drawer and cut her long curls until she was left with a very short pixie. The look was shockingly different, but maybe attractive in a new way. Who would be interested in a woman undergoing chemo? A woman with hair like this? Jenny forced these worries from her head and prepared herself to see Dr. Scott.

He complimented her on her new style, and asked if she was ready to set up the next operation.

She sighed. "What is the surgery for this time?"

Dr. Scott explained the surgery was to remove the tumors in her breasts. "Some surgeons, like Dr. Emory, prefer to remove everything, but in my experience, most of my patients don't want that. This surgeon will only remove what is necessary. He is brilliant with reconstruction, too."

Tears welled in Jenny's eyes, but she was resigned to the surgery. With a sorrowful look, she told him to set it up.

Dr. Scott confessed, "I've already spoken to the surgeon, and he agrees with the minimally invasive approach. After we finish chemo, we'll get things going."

Jenny nodded.

"In the meantime, Jenny, I have someone else I would really like you to meet." Dr. Scott paused. "He's a friend that I send a lot of my people to. He's a doctor that works with people suffering from depression."

Jenny's tone changed. "A psychiatrist? Are you kidding? You think I'm crazy, now?"

Dr. Scott took her hand. "Look, this is a lot to handle. It's okay to admit you need some help. I can see you're upset, but you need to consider how your emotions can work together with your body to affect the outcome of your treatment."

She stood, yanked her hand away, and glared at him. "So, you think I somehow need your help? That I'm too crazy to handle this on my own?" Jenny pushed a chair out of her path and left the office.

Dr. Scott followed her to the parking area and stopped her from leaving. "Look, Jenny, I didn't mean to make you feel bad. I don't think you're crazy. I simply want to help you. I hate seeing you so unhappy all the time. I'm concerned for you. So often, it seems like you're overcome with emotions. I thought that maybe talking to someone would help. That's all."

"Maybe I just won't come back for any more treatments, if I'm worrying everyone so much," Jenny said. "I don't need anything. I don't need therapy."

Jenny swung open her car door and dodged to get inside.

Dr. Scott stopped her in her tracks by gently grabbing her hand. "Wait, calm down. Just stop for a second, and let's talk this through," he pleaded with her.

"What more do you want to say?" Jenny snapped back.

"I don't understand why you're so angry with me. I'm just trying to help."

"I don't need to be pitied," Jenny said. "I need to be free. Free of pain and free from being poked and probed with needles."

"That will come in time, Jenny," Dr. Scott reassured her. "But while you're in treatment, I want you to know there are people and resources to support you through this. You don't have to face it alone."

"Why do you want to help me so much? Don't you have hundreds of other patients?" Jenny questioned his intentions.

"Well, yes..." The doctor stammered. "Look, there may be more to this. I shouldn't even be admitting this, but Jenny, I've adored you since the first day I met you. It's inappropriate on so many levels, I know, but there's something about you I can't resist."

Jenny collapsed on a nearby bench, and Dr. Scott took a seat at least a foot away from her.

"I left my clinic and followed you," he said, "because you're intoxicating to me. I want to be around you all day, every day."

"So, now what?" Jenny asked.

"I don't expect you to marry me, okay? Just let me help you. Forget about the psychiatrist thing, and let's start over. I'll listen when you need to talk, and I'll be a shoulder when you need one to cry on. What do you say?"

"I've had terrible things happen to me, and most of it was my own fault. I'm dealing with it. If you really want to help me, be patient and let me figure things out," Jenny said.

Dr. Scott agreed to wait, and they returned to the clinic, so Jenny could gather her purse and head home.

A month passed. Her surgery was finished. The method Dr. Scott recommended only removed part of the breast and rebuilt it to look almost perfect. He assured her that they had gotten all the cancer. His feelings for Jenny had grown, but he only told her he wanted her to be happy with the results.

She was weaker now and very pale. Her thin frame was clothed in textured outfits, and she chose decorative scarves to cover her head. She went back to college to tutor some of her former students, but wasn't ready to face a classroom of peers or professors. She imagined the pitying stares. It was just too much to explain. She was weaker with every treatment, but she had more hope than before.

During a round of chemo, she was walking the hospital halls and ran into the guy she'd met at Sarah's party. "James? Is that you?" she asked. James had worked construction for Michael's father for a while during his senior year. He was always tanned and had a great build. She only knew that because he constantly walked around without his shirt, showing off his abs.

Now here he was, thin and pale, being pushed around in a wheelchair. He was also in his final round of chemo, fighting stage four liver cancer. She barely recognized him. They were so happy to see each other and spent hours in the lobby atrium catching up. "So much for the goddess of beauty, huh?" James teased her.

Jenny rubbed her scarf and laughed. "Yeah well, I take it you haven't looked in a mirror lately," she teased back. It was the first time she had laughed in forever. No one but another cancer patient could understand and tease with laughter instead of hurt feelings.

"Who's here with you?"

"Nobody. In fact, nobody knows I'm here. They don't even know I'm sick. I've cut all ties. Please don't tell anyone that you saw me here," Jenny begged. It was a relief to reveal herself to someone who understood.

James kept teasing. "Not like I'm gonna run out and call the press. I'm just glad you're here with me. I mean, I'm sorry you're sick, but I love the company." He kissed her hand. "This is the best I've felt in a while."

The next morning, Michael was at the hospital visiting James. Michael's family knew how bad off James was and helped to make sure he had the best of care. Michael was upset when he saw how his friend was feeling. It was obvious that the end was near. He walked the long hallway. There were many rooms, and several nurses and doctors passed him with purposeful strides.

Jenny had left her room to see James. She pushed her IV pole, as she shuffled her slipper socks along, staring at the gray tiled floor, a little wobbly and afraid of tripping.

Michael walked toward her on the other side. He looked at the woman walking slowly, and he stopped to stare. He was amazed how much this woman resembled Jenny. At that moment, she looked up and caught his eye. His breath caught in his throat. His beautiful girl stood there, pale and skinny, her lustrous curls gone. He walked to her and took her hand so gently, as if she might break. "Cancer?" he asked, his voice shaking.

She nodded yes, unable to speak. He put his arms around her. She was safe. She sobbed against his chest, and he cried along with her. He helped her back to her bed, and she couldn't stop looking at him.

"Why didn't you call me? Or Jack? He's been as worried as I have."

"It was all too much. I didn't want anyone to know. I couldn't take people seeing me this way, feeling sorry for me. Especially you. But you found me."

Michael told her he came to visit James. "For all the times I've spent searching for you, I finally found you when I wasn't looking." He kissed her hand so long and so gently.

"I'm not a weakling, silly." She tried to tease like the old Jenny he knew. The whirling sensation she felt wasn't due to her treatment. She kissed his cheek.

Michael told her how serious James's condition was. He listened to Jenny talk about the hours she'd spent with James in the atrium and how they'd lifted one another's spirits.

"I'm afraid he told you the truth," Michael said about James's jokes. "It's not just his weird sense of humor. He really is dying."

He searched her face, looking for answers. Holding her hand, he didn't want to let go. "I still don't get it. Why didn't you call me? You know I would've been here in a minute."

"I know you would have, that's exactly why I didn't. I told you I was no good for you. I wasn't about to saddle you with a dying woman."

Michael kissed her forehead. "You aren't dying. Don't say that."

"You just don't understand," she cried. "I needed to see this through alone."

"Alone? Where's the asshole?" Michael's tension raised his voice before he remembered where they were. "Why isn't he here?" He waited.

It took her a minute to gather her words. She sat up straighter and started, "Richard is gone. I haven't seen him in months. He hurt me, Michael. He was only after my money. It was a game, I guess. I'm not sure how. He lured me in, robbed me blind, raped me, beat me, tortured me, and if I hadn't gotten sick, he probably would have killed me."

Her story was out, not the way she'd intended, but it was time. "It's over. He's gone. From my hospital bed, I filed for divorce, and it will be final soon."

Michael stood with clenched fists and paced the small hospital room. "I can't believe you didn't tell us what he did to you. He could've—the fucking bastard—where is he now? I will seriously kill him."

She shook her head. "And end up in jail? Not a good idea. Besides, he's either in another country—Mexico maybe, on my money—or he's in jail. Either way, he's out of my life. He had no idea where I went or if I died. Let it go. I'm working on doing just that."

Michael went back to the bed and sat next to her. He took her in his arms and told her she was right. All that mattered now was that she was safe, and they were together. He promised her he would take her home with him and take care of her after she was released. "No more staying alone. No more dumping me."

"Michael, I can't listen to this. I'm not whole. I'll only cause you more worry and heartache than when I was gone from your life."

They argued until Michael finally had enough. "Can you just stop arguing? It's been a crazy hard day, and we're both a little off." He kissed her forehead and lingered at the nearness of her. "There is time," he assured her. "I'm here now, and I'm not going anywhere."

She closed her eyes and laid her head back. Despite James's desperate situation, she allowed herself this moment of contentment.

Later that night, James was feeling bad, and he was afraid that he'd die alone in his room. He thought about Jenny and snuck out of his room to find her. He stumbled into her room where she was asleep. He walked in and kissed her forehead. She woke up, startled.

"James. Are you alright?" She asked frantically. He crawled into the bed next to her.

"I didn't want to be alone. I'm scared. Do you mind?" "Of course not." She pulled the blanket up over his shoulders.

"You're my angel, Jen. I hope you know that." Jenny shushed him. "I do, James, I really do. Everything is going to be okay. I promise." She hoped her voice sounded more convincing than she felt.

Morning came and Jenny's nurse saw James in bed next to Jenny. She opened the blinds to wake them. The sun came beaming in. She noticed James's color and rushed to him. He was already gone. Jenny woke up and screamed.

She was terrified to see James dead right next to her. When they came to take his body, she was still screaming and crying. Dr. Scott came in and tried to make her go back to her bed, but she was still shaking and frightened.

Dr. Scott explained what had happened. James was very sick, and they knew he would die any minute. He tried to comfort her with the cold, hard facts.

She was so upset that she'd lost yet another friend. Michael came in as Dr. Scott was trying to get Jenny to understand the dire situation James had been in.

"What's going on?" he asked.

Jenny looked up at him. "Oh Michael, it's James. He died in my bed."

Michael couldn't make sense of what she was saying.

He kept wiping her tears.

"He was here," she told him pointing to the right side of her mattress. "He was so afraid to be alone, so he got in bed with me."

He hugged her while she shook. Dr. Scott called the nurses for sedation. Michael stayed until she dropped off to sleep, and then Dr. Scott asked Michael if he could talk to him in the hallway. "Are you a relative? Jenny told me she was alone."

Michael told him that he had only yesterday learned she was sick.

Dr. Scott was worried that Michael was the one who had abused her so badly. "We have a responsibility to protect our patients—"

"Look Doc, I'm the good guy here. Her husband was the one who hurt her. I didn't know where she was. I'm in love with her and don't intend to ever let anyone hurt her again."

Dr. Scott was convinced and agreed to let her go home with him.

Michael took Jenny to his house, and she was grateful for the help. When he eased her into a chair, he noticed a chain around her neck. "What's that?" he said.

Jenny showed him the ring he'd given her at the bottom of the chain.

"You know how that makes me feel?" he said. He knelt in front of her chair. "I know you're not done with your treatments, and with everything that's happened, it's too soon to make any decisions." He held the ring on its chain. "But even if your treatments aren't over, let's think about starting a life together."

"Oh Michael, how can you even think that way?" she said. "With everything that's happened to me, I'm even worse for you than I was before. Why would you want to marry me just to watch me die?"

"No. I'm going to watch you live."

"Can you do one thing for me? Please don't tell my family. You can tell them you saw me, but they need to think I'm fine and that everything is good," she begged.

Michael hesitated. "One thing," he said. "You do me a favor, too. Please call your brother. He's so worried about you. Let him know you've forgiven him. He feels so guilty about your argument, and he thinks that's why you left."

"I can't do that Michael," she said "I can't hear his voice."

Michael didn't want to force her to do something that she couldn't do, so he didn't ask her for more.

Jenny stayed at Michael's house and continued her therapy. She still had to go through more treatments, and she was worried the cancer would turn up somewhere else. She was sick from the chemo, and her depression was getting the best of her.

Michael tried everything to make her feel better. He was taking care of her and never left her side, even for a minute. He had to cut back his hours at the office to take care of her, but he was willing to give up everything for her so she could get well.

But deep down, Jenny was certain she was going to die like Hanna did, and she didn't want to put him through that suffering. She convinced herself that she had to break it off with Michael permanently. She made plans to go back to her apartment near the hospital. This disease was not going to let go of her any time soon, and she felt guilty to have this great guy give up his chance at a happy life because she was robbed of hers. It was selfish.

Michael, on the other hand, wouldn't hear of it. They argued, and every time she tried to convince him that letting her go was the right thing to do. He wouldn't budge.

On the day Jenny left the hospital, Michael immediately hopped on the subject again. He wanted her forever, and he wouldn't take no for an answer. But Jenny had prepared herself for this. She would be adamant; Michael would have to start a new life, one that didn't include her. She would only cause him sorrow.

She sat on their bed and patted the spot next to her, signaling Michael to come over. Instead, he grabbed a chair and sat directly in front of her. He liked to feel as if he was in control, even if Jenny was the ultimate decision maker.

"Michael, we have to talk," Jenny said. She knew these were the four most soul-crushing words to anyone who loved another. "You need to let me go now, so it won't be as hard on you when I die later."

"What are you talking about, Jenny?" Michael was furious. "The doctor said there was hope, you have time." He paced the room in anger.

"Can't you see that I'm getting worse every single day?" she said. "I'm suffering enough; you don't have to, as well."

Michael got down on his knees, hung his head over her lap, and held her hands.

"I won't suffer," he promised. "If I let you go, I won't have anything to live for. It's simply impossible for me to do what you're asking."

Jenny laid her back against the headboard feeling defeated and exhausted. "I've already taken too much of your time. I'll only feel more guilty the longer you take care of me."

She wanted to die alone. "I'm dying, Michael. But the guilt of holding you back is killing me quicker than the sickness. You deserve to build a life with a stable woman. To have kids and a home you can share with someone who loves you completely. Don't you want that?"

"I do," Michael said. "But I want it with you."

By now, Michael was outraged. He finally had her in his home, the home he built for her, and all she wanted to do was escape.

"This isn't a game," Michael shouted. "I'm not a toy you can pick up whenever you're bored and put down when you aren't. I mean nothing to you." "You don't understand what it's like to have cancer, to be told you might have an expiration date on your life."

Michael wasn't satisfied by Jenny's explanation. His eyes filled with tears, and the sight pulled at her heartstrings. She ran her fingers through his hair, and he lifted her, spun her around, and sat her back gently on the bed.

"I care about you," she said after a few minutes. "I may be dying, but you have to live. Marry someone who will make you happy. Promise me
that you'll do that."

"I can't imagine myself with anyone but you," Michael said, and he rolled his fists into giant balls. With one quick uppercut, he pierced a hole in the wall.

Jenny knew this would only escalate, so she pulled out her last remaining defense. "Michael, I don't want you, okay?" And as she said it, although she only half believed it, she thrust the necklace with his ring on it to the ground.

He understood what her action meant. This was her final goodbye.

"Please go," she said with a sureness that broke Michael's heart into pieces.

He stormed out of the room, and as he made his way out the door, he demolished all of the furniture, vases, and picture frames in his path.

One day, he'll realize this was for the best, Jenny thought. Or at least she hoped.

Weeks passed by without a word from Jenny. Michael replayed her argument in his mind. When he returned home to find her gone, he could do nothing except pick up the shards of glass and splinters of wood from his destruction. He spent his time working too much, and in his empty house, drinking too much.

One day, when he'd just gotten home, Jenny's father called. What he hoped would be good news ended up with an all-out rush to the hospital, careening around corners, and running stoplights.

Jack had an accident at work and was badly burned. Michael ran in the door and saw Jack's parents. His mom came to Michael, hugging and weeping, keening back and forth. Jack was all she had left. Michael held her close, but his eyes searched for Jenny. Jack's mother returned to his side to hold his good hand. Nurses came and went, checking signs.

Jenny burst into the room and went straight to Jack. No one else in the room existed for her. "I'm here, bud," she whispered. "You didn't have to go do stupid shit like this to get me to come." She looked for a place to hug, but the burns covered his body. She held his hand.

Jack squeezed her hand tightly to let her know he heard her.

"I love you, too," she cried softly. His hand went limp, and the monitor alarm beeped a long, never-ending tone that pierced her heart. He wouldn't make it. Another person had been hijacked from Jenny's life.

Jack's limp body appeared serene on the hospital bed. Jenny looked past the severe burns and into his eyes. At least he wasn't suffering anymore, that was the only relief she could cling to.

The family gathered in the waiting room, reeling from the events that had just occurred. As the adrenaline subsided and the grief set in, her parents finally realized the change in their dear Jenny. It was all out in the open now. In her rush to get to the hospital, she hadn't worn a scarf. Her hair was barely beginning to grow back. They knew she was recovering from cancer. She brought them up to speed and tried to comfort her mother. She knew they were upset already and didn't want to add to their despair.

The funeral was a few days later. To Jenny, burying Jack was like burying a piece of herself. Her DNA was six feet under, and in many ways, she felt dead, too. She visited Jack's grave, which wasn't far from Oliver's, and she cried until the tears stopped.

Michael put his hand on the small of her back. But seconds later, she was on the soft, green grass, sobbing into her palms. Drops of rain pattered against the black umbrella that Michael held over her head. He kneeled down and cried alongside her.

"Do you wanna come home with me?" he asked.

She nodded yes. Loss was exhausting, and Jenny could feel it in her bones. She couldn't muster the energy to stand, so Michael draped her arms around his shoulder and carried her to his car.

In silence, they drove back to his house. When they walked through the front door, Michael wasted no time. He knew where Jenny wanted to be and hauled her up the spiral staircase to the bedroom. With diligence, he peeled each muddy, soaking layer of clothing off her body. While he meant well, Jenny wasn't in the mood.

"I don't know why I agreed to come here," she sighed. She tried to contain her emotions, but in an instant, she was crying.

"Why does everyone I know or love die, Michael? Hanna, Oliver, and now Jack. It's like I'm cursed, a bad luck charm or something."

"Death is a natural part of life, Jenny. You know that. Everyone has his or her day, and it's not a result of anything you do or say. Don't cry, baby, please," Michael said.

She knew he was right, but turned her face away from him anyway.

Michael caught a glimpse of her back, which was still scarred from Richard's torture. Michael wrapped a blanket around Jenny's body. He didn't want to see the reminders of Richard. That lowlife had really done a number on her.

"Maybe you should take a shower," Michael suggested. "It might make you feel better."

She didn't really feel like cleaning herself. She wasn't ready to erase the remnants of the graveyard just yet. But she decided that Michael may have a point and grabbed a robe and towel.

After she stepped out of the shower, she immersed herself within the folds of Michael's large robe and sipped hot tea from her usual mug. The two of them talked for a while about nothing in particular, each finding comfort in the sound of the other's voice.

He brought in her clothes from the dryer and set them on the chair.

She looked at them and then back at him. "It's probably best that I leave soon."

"I've already called a taxi. It's ready when you are," Michael said passively. He knew the drill at this point and figured now wasn't the time to push his own agenda. He finished his drink as she headed out the door.

Chapter Four

Jenny tried to return to some version of normalcy. She was back to taking online classes, but wasn't quite ready to face a room full of students who would all remind her of Jack. Like Hanna, he'd never walk into another room, let alone a classroom, again. She tried not to remember the burns, the grave, and the wilting flowers that surrounded it.

But she couldn't help but think that she would be next.

She was still going through chemo, so she rarely had the time or energy to meet up with Michael.

Michael didn't want to move on or pursue any interests. There was his work, and that was it. To appease his mother, he attended an event at her house. It was a crowded, formal affair with lots of guests. He turned from his spot on the balcony to see a woman approach him wearing a daring evening gown, carrying two glasses. It was Christa, a woman his mother had told him about.

She handed him one of the glasses and tried to strike up a conversation. "It feels good out here." Michael looked up and nodded. He had no intention of engaging her, but Michael was nothing if not a gentleman. Refusing to be rude or disrespectful, he took a big gulp of his whiskey and stood up. "The breeze is nice for sure," he added.

Christa moved closer. "Why so glum?" she asked. "Glum? There's a word."

"I've seen you a few times, and you always look like you just lost your best friend. Why are you so sad?" She nudged his arm.

"That's because I did." He chugged the rest of his drink and went inside. Christa followed him and watched him say goodbye to his mother." He kissed her cheek and left.

"So, what's his problem? Is he with someone? He just blew me off like I didn't exist." Christa wasn't used to being ignored.

His mother watched him drive away through the window. "No, he isn't with anyone. He just has a broken heart; a goddess is what he calls her." She sighed, and left Christa standing alone.

The day Jenny had waited for arrived, at last. When the receptionist ushered her into the doctor's private office instead of the usual exam room, her anxiety flared. Dr. Scott rushed in and flopped her chart on the desk, startling her. "I have some news for you, my dear," he began. "The scans are showing no regrowth, and the blood work is improving." He waited for her to react. She didn't. "Did you not hear me?" he asked.

"I heard you. What does that mean exactly?"

"It means the treatments worked. We'll scan regularly to watch it, but if there's nothing in six months, you'll be considered cancer free." He sat back in his chair and folded his arms.

Jenny couldn't believe what she was hearing, afraid to get her hopes up. "Has this ever happened before?" she asked.

Dr. Scott assured her it had. It was not common, but because they found hers so early and treated it so aggressively, he believed it could be true.

She unleashed a smile and thanked him with a heartfelt hug and kiss on his cheek. "You're a miracle worker," she said.

Jenny went home that night, and the world looked brighter. The clouds over her future were clearing away, and she was happy. It felt like the time to start putting her life back together. There was hope for the first time in so long.

Michael was attending his cousin's wedding with his family. Over two hundred elegantly dressed people mingled around the glittering ballroom. Christa caught sight of him standing at the open bar and made her way to him. "Can I join you, or is it alone time?"

He raised his glass and said hello. "A friend of the bride or groom?"

"I saw that your little buddy hit the dance floor and left you alone. I figured I'd come chat you up...do you not dance?"

Michael looked at Christa, set his empty glass on the bar, and took her hand, leading her to the dance floor without a word. Christa was thrilled, but Michael was deep inside his head. He remembered dancing with Jenny, spinning her around the room. Where was she at that moment? Did she need him? Did she miss him at all?

The music ended, and he walked back to the bar. Christa followed close behind. If he ordered another whiskey, maybe she would find someone else to talk to. Drinking might be the perfect solution. Yet she stayed. Christa relentlessly bombarded him with questions, but he had tuned her out. He finally tried to be polite and listen to her.

"So, do you live alone?" he inquired.

"In many ways, yes, but not technically," she said with a vagueness that confused Michael.

"What do you mean?"

"I live with my parents," she explained, and sipped her wine.

"Why?" he asked harshly.

She told him that with her parents' wealth and power, there was no need for her to move out and live alone.

Their house was big enough. She rambled on for a long time, practically telling him her life story. He interrupted her at one point.

"So, let me get this right. You don't work, you didn't go to college, and you really have no plans for the future. Tell me Christa, what do you do with your life?"

She was mildly offended by his remark. "I do plenty, thank you. I volunteer a lot. I never saw the need for a formal education. I'm smart enough." She flashed him a smile.

Christa didn't think he liked her answer, and she was mute for a moment as she tried to come up with another angle. "Everybody is different, my dear. Different isn't always a bad thing."

"Yes, I suppose you're right," Michael said, sarcastically. How could two women be so different?

"By the way," Christa started, abruptly changing the subject. "Rumor has it you loved a goddess once."

"Yes, and…?" Michael replied.

"Well, tell me about her. What makes her a goddess?" He turned his head, put his glass on a table beside him, and flashed a piercing glance at Christa that shot through her soul. "Because, like you said, everybody is different, and that's how she is. She's different. She's a goddess."

Without another word, he left Christa by the bar shocked, unsatisfied, and alone.

Jenny was, in fact, getting better. Dr. Scott was happy to see her improvement. She beat the disease, and she had a new outlook. Maybe she was able to work through her malignant spirits on her own. Jenny knew that he'd helped her make it this far. He put up with a lot of her crap along the way. So, when he invited her to dinner to celebrate, she accepted gratefully.

He took her to a restaurant by the lake, and she loved the view from their lakeside table. Jenny thanked him and told him how lucky she felt to have him as her doctor. "I know I was a pain in the ass, and I'm sorry for giving you such a hard time," she said.

Dr. Scott was glad she was enjoying herself, but hoped that a lakeside dinner would be a romantic beginning that would lead to something more. He realized quickly that her gestures of appreciation for his care were all about his role as her doctor, nothing more. He hid his disappointment, and they had a pleasant enough evening, laughing and swapping stories.

At the end of the evening, he dropped her off at home. She thanked him for dinner, pecked his cheek, and hopped out of the car. "See you at my next appointment," she called as he drove off.

Michael fell into the habit of drinking. He practiced his new habits of drowning his sorrows and partying every chance he got. Taxi drivers knew him by name from his multiple pick-ups at the local bars.

His mother was worried when she saw him with his friends at her party. After drinking all night, his friends had left.

It was getting late, and Christa saw him sitting on the deck with his eyes closed and his head leaning back on the wall. "Hey, you all right?"

Michael opened one eye and saw who it was. "I'm fine."

"Would you like some water?" she asked.

"No, I have whiskey. What the hell would I do with water?" Michael looked at the sky and loosened his tie.

Christa moved closer to him and put her drink on the table. She bent down and kissed Michael's lips.

He opened his eyes and looked at her face. "What are you doing, Christa?"

She giggled. "I just couldn't resist, sorry."

Michael slurred, "I'm a bad guy; you shouldn't kiss me."

Christa moved closer and put her thigh between his knees. She ran her fingers through his hair. She kissed him again, and this time he pulled her down to sit on his lap.

Christa put her finger on his lips. "Just shush." She kissed his neck and nibbled his earlobes until he pushed her away.

"Please stop this," he pleaded. "It isn't a good idea."

She continued her seductive moves, and he tried his best to resist her. He had no feelings for this woman, and in his drunken state, he couldn't understand why she would not go away. She started unbuttoning his shirt and kissing his chest, moving down toward his belt. When she started to unbuckle it, he grabbed her hand. "I cannot do this," he said firmly.

She pouted and made him feel bad, as if it was his fault. He didn't want to hurt her feelings, but she was not Jenny. Christa finished her wine and straddled his lap, reaching around to kiss his neck. Her breath was hot in his ear. Jenny had told him to move on with his life, and here was this woman practically begging him to jump her. He took her hand and led her to the guest room in the back.

"What the hell," he thought. As the door closed, they began tearing at each other's clothes. There was nothing romantic about any of this. He pinned her against the wall, and she was all over him. She was a maniac, or he was just really drunk. They ended up on the bed somehow, and she screamed underneath him. He wasn't sure if he was hurting her or if she was just that into it.

Afterwards, Christa slid off the bed to sit on the floor.

She looked at Michael, but he was already passed out.

Dr. Scott couldn't stop thinking about the date. He scolded himself for chickening out. Halfway home, he turned around and went back to Jenny's apartment. She opened the door and looked baffled. Holding up his hand, he told her, "Before you say anything, I want you to know that I had planned tonight to be special. I was hoping you and I could take this relationship to another level. Not doctor/patient or friends that celebrate together, but a couple, two people who care about each other. I wanted it to be the beginning, and I feel like it fizzled."

She laughed. "Can I speak now?" she asked. He nodded.

"Fizzled? Really?" What does that mean?"

He looked down, embarrassed. "I'm afraid I'd be letting a chance slip by, if I didn't tell you how I feel," he said.

She didn't know what to say. She'd always been attracted to him, but never thought of him in that way. "You're my doctor," she blurted.

"What's your point? I'm a man. You're a woman. Why can't we just see where it goes?"

She told him she was worried about getting involved and how it might affect their professional relationship.

"It doesn't matter, Jenny."

She leaned in and kissed him. "Want to come in for a night cap?" she asked.

When Dr. Scott left, she undressed as she walked to her room and flopped down on her bed. She stared at the ceiling for a while, remembering the first time she met him and all their time together since. Why hadn't she seen it? Was it there all along? Her mind swirled.

Michael was having a hard time faking it. Even his friends noticed the changes—his anger, the way he snapped at everyone for no reason. He spent his down time drinking alone. But wherever he turned, Christa seemed to show up. And Michael was fed up with her.

Visits with his family became less frequent after they told him to stop drinking. He pretended his simple routine worked for him. He went to work, came home, drank until he was tired, and went to bed. How could he possibly start up with another woman? The pillow Jenny slept on was the one he'd slept with, for God's sake. It had a trace of her perfume on it.

Christa visited him at his office one day. She just showed up as if somehow that was okay.

Michael was really irritated. "What are you doing here?" he snapped.

She shot him a look. "It's been over a month, and I haven't heard from you? What the hell is going on?" she asked.

"What do you mean what's going on. I owe you something? I'm pretty sure I made it clear that I wasn't interested."

"So, what was that? A quick one-night piece? Classy." She paced the office floor, her heels clicking on the wood.

Michael came from behind the desk and stopped her with his hands on her shoulders. "Listen. I don't know what you imagined was going to happen here, but I told you from the start that I'm not interested. I am in love with another woman. I have no intention of being with you. Not now. Not ever. I mean, shit, I never led you on. I was almost rude about it, I...."

"Michael, I'm pregnant." She sat down and covered her face to hide her tears.

Michael just stared at her. He felt like he'd been kicked in the gut. A thousand questions flashed through his mind, and he tried to find words for the one he wanted to ask most.

"Is it—?"

"Of course it's yours. What do you think I am?"

He led her to the door. "Just go home. We'll talk tonight. I have a meeting, and I can't deal with this right now." He closed the door behind her. Once she was in the hall, he walked back to his chair and slammed his fists on the desk so hard that it shook.

Jenny and Dr. Scott had seen each other a few times, not only at her appointments, but for a couple of casual dinner dates. She knew he was a good man, and she enjoyed his company, but there were really no feelings for him. But she was starting to look like herself again and felt like getting out more.

Her hair was growing in to the point where people on the street didn't blink and look away when they saw her. Her color was no longer pale, and she was feeling so much better. To look at her, nobody would believe what she had been through. She even smiled.

On the way to see Christa, Michael was trying to sort out what she'd told him. Pregnant. Unbelievable. He thought of Jenny and wondered if she was even still alive. Would he know if something happened to her? She always told him to be happy and make a life, but this wasn't the life he wanted.

As he pulled into the long curve of Christa's driveway, he made his decision. It was clear that he would never be happy again, but he could at least do the right thing. He was waiting in the front room, slamming down his Jack and Coke as fast as possible when she came down.

"They said I had a visitor, but I didn't think it would be you."

"I told you we'd talk tonight." His voice was emotionless. He finished his drink and took a ring out of his pocket. He held it out and she took it.

"What's this for?" she asked.

"We'll get married. I'll buy you a house. We'll raise the baby." His voice sounded like he was giving directions at a construction site.

She was less than impressed with his proposal. "What about your *goddess*? I thought she was the only one for you."

"Please don't. Don't do that," he said quietly. It pained him to tell her about Jenny's disease. "Hell, for all I know she may be dead already." He laughed bitterly. Then, he began to cry.

Christa was upset seeing this strong man so broken, so undone by this emotional upheaval. She tried to comfort him, meeting him on the ground when he collapsed to his knees. His body shuddered under the grief, and within Christa's arms, he seemed small like a child.

"It's cancer," he said.

Christa shook her head. She'd never met Jenny, and she didn't like her, but cancer? At least she could be secure in the knowledge that Michael might be hers forever. And with that glimmer of hope, she indulged his tears and patted his back until he fell asleep.

As if she'd been planning it since she was a child, Christa put together a huge, formal wedding within weeks. No detail was overlooked.

Michael had relished the idea of planning a wedding once, too, but it involved a different bride. He was not excited, nor all that invested, or impressed with Christa's grandiose affair. Although he tried to hide his feelings, a depressed drunk is obvious to everyone. His mother stepped in for him, coordinating the catering service, floral arrangements, and even selecting the wedding cake Michael and Christa would jointly cut into during the reception.

It was as if Michael had only been invited to someone else's wedding and not preparing for his own. He bought her a fancy home and was at her beck and call, so he figured he paid his dues in other areas.

The ceremony was beautiful, and Christa was radiant.

As the pastor spoke, Michael fantasized about Jenny standing next to him. He heard nothing. No music. No words. Christa squeezed his hand, as it was his turn to say *I do*. He looked startled and answered as he was expected to.

After the show was over and they were back at the house, Christa showered and put on her sexiest nightgown. When she entered the bedroom, she was surprised to find it empty. She searched the huge house and found Michael on the bed in the back room.

"What are you doing in here?"

"Trying to sleep."

She knew he was drunk, but wasn't expecting him to be an ass on their wedding night. "Okay, why in here?"

"Because this is my room." He pointed down the hall. "And that is your room…go to it."

She argued, "Seriously? Why are you…?"

He jumped up, pointed toward her room, and screamed at her, "Go. Leave me the fuck alone."

Christa was shocked at Michael's attitude on their wedding night. She hurried to her room and slammed the door.

Through the small-town grapevine, Jenny found out about Michael's marriage. The news devastated her, but she realized that he was only doing what she'd asked him to do. Still, it cut through her like a knife. She decided to take her mind off things by studying a little extra than normal and pampering herself with a manicure and massage.

She looked better, but regret bubbled like tar inside her chest. He deserved this new life; one that didn't include her. And that's what she told herself for the seven days leading up to the event.

The evening of Michael's wedding, Jenny and Dr. Scott had been out dancing. They went to his house afterwards for a drink. Jenny had made up her mind that she needed to move on with her life, too. When Dr. Scott made his move, as he had done a few times now, Jenny didn't shut him down. Instead, she put Michael out of her head and gave in. Dr. Scott was much different than the other men she'd been with. He was gentle and sweet. He didn't *have sex* with her; he *made love* to her. Dr. Scott knew her feelings, but he loved her. For him, it was enough.

A couple of months passed, and Jenny graduated from college. She chose to celebrate the achievement alone.

She'd wanted to do many things in her life, mainly travel, but everything had changed. Michael was married, and even if she wanted him now more than ever, he couldn't be hers.

Hadn't she told him to move on? Surely this undamaged woman was best for him. She didn't want to know who his wife was, but a part of her wished she was the one who had said "I do." But yet, she was still wearing his ring, and a ring is forever.

Later that night, Dr. Scott visited Jenny. "Congratulations, Jenny."

She turned, frosting covered knife in her hand, to see who was talking to her.

"Whoa. I come in peace. I'm bearing gifts." Dr. Scott laughed. He handed her a box. "Open it."

To her relief, the box was too big for a ring. She lifted the top and saw a crown of small flowers, just big enough to encircle her hair. She pulled it out and put it on. "How sweet you are." She beamed.

He took the knife from her hand and put it on the table. "Let's celebrate," he said.

Jenny spent the first weeks after graduation filling out online applications for work-study graduate courses for Italy. One afternoon, she reached into the mailbox and pulled out the manila envelope she'd been waiting for from the Department of State. She ripped it open in anticipation and flipped up the navy-blue folder. Staring back at her was her smiling passport picture.

The first thing she thought to do was grab her phone to share the excitement with Sarah. But instead, the phone rang in her hand. Jenny's mother was in tears. Her father had passed away. She rushed to her mother, and the two of them immersed themselves in the upheaval that comes with a funeral. Through the preparations and notifications, they focused only on what they had to do.

It wasn't until after the service was over, and the loved ones left with hugs and condolences, that they sat and looked at each other. Here was the hard part, the grief and loss. It had become second nature to her family, but that reality didn't make the process easier.

Jenny spent the next few weeks helping her mom and wandering through the quiet house. They read the condolence cards with their messages of comfort, including one from Michael. Like Michael with her pillow, she slept in her dad's bed, holding his robe. It smelled like him and made her feel like a little girl again.

Her father's death sent Jenny into a tailspin. He had been her Superman. There was never a question he didn't have the answer to, and he always knew how to make Jenny happy.

Sarah came over often, and they told her stories of childhood memories. Memories of her childhood soccer games—he'd never missed one—and summer vacations to the cabin on the lake came to mind and magnified the loss. A darkness took over. She stopped eating and sleeping, and her health began to deteriorate. Dr.

Scott came to check on her and reminded her how fragile her system still was. She didn't care.

One night, in a desperate frame of mind, she went to her father's closet and found his old revolver. She struggled to see through her tears and loaded it. As she held it to her heart and tried to get the nerve to pull the trigger, she thought of her dad. How disappointed he would be in her. She could almost hear him telling her to think of her mother. Who would be left to care for her?

She knew she couldn't put her mother rough that, too.

She put the gun down and cried herself to sleep.

In the morning, Jenny woke to see the gun still on the pillow next to her. "What was I thinking?" she whispered.

She unloaded the gun and put it back in the lockbox on the shelf in the closet. She passed the mirror and forced a smile, brushing the hair out of her eyes. "Enough," she said. "Get your shit together. You're stronger than this."

Her priority had to be to take care of her mom and keep the family business profitable. They relocated the business office closer to home, where she could be with her mother every day.

Travel plans returned to travel dreams. Her passport was pushed to the back of a drawer.

"It's a girl." Michael heard the doctor say. The baby was here, and she was beautiful. Michael was finally able to love again. That tiny human had stolen his heart. As the days went by and he saw what a loving mom Christa was to his little angel, Michael started to appreciate his wife a little more.

They still had separate bedrooms, but there were nights spent together when the mood struck. Nights at the bar were less frequent, and Michael tried to get his drinking under control.

Both of them were surprised that Michael willingly changed diapers in the middle of sleepless nights and listened to the pediatrician during appointments. After work, when he weighed the possibility of going to the bar or going home to tell baby Lauren about his day, he chose the baby more often than not. He bored people at the office with videos on his phone of her first babbles and her first time pulling herself to her feet.

One cold Monday morning, Michael was trying to catch up on work that his office staff had missed while he was away in Lansing. He came across a check made out to Alan's Landscaping. He tracked down his secretary to find out what it was written for.

"I don't see the issue, we've paid them for years," she said.

"I know, but they closed months ago, after the old man died, right?"

"No, sir. They moved, but they're still operating. I believe his daughter is running it now."

Michael froze.

He drove past the old place on his way home and read the sign in the window giving the address of the new location. The next day, he took Christa shopping near the Alan's new shop. He busied her looking for baby clothes and wheeled the stroller to the building across the street.

He opened the door, clearly marked with Jenny's name, and saw her sitting at the computer in the corner, her back to him. As he stepped in front of the stroller, she turned, almost in slow motion, and their eyes met. He couldn't believe the blush in her cheeks, her hair. He walked closer.

"Jenny. You're here," he said in amazement. He cleared his throat.

"Michael," she gave him a sad smile.

As he got closer, he could smell a hint of her perfume.

A surge of memories rushed to mind. "You look so...normal. I mean like five years younger." "It's surprising how being cancer free makes me feel.

Actually, I'm doing great."

Michael had questions that tumbled over each other about where she'd been and how she'd come to take over the family business, when the baby he was carrying began crying. He pointed to Jenny. "Jenny, I'd like you to meet Lauren." He paused. "My daughter."

Jenny gulped hard. "Wow," she said. Her shock at Michael's presence had made her overlook the stroller. "She's beautiful. What a little miracle."

"This is a miracle, seeing you healthy. Look at you. You truly are a goddess." He leaned out the door and waved for Christa to come over and join him. When Christa walked in the office, he handed her the baby. "Jenny this is Christa...my wife. Christa, this is Jenny, the woman I love." Jenny was shocked by Michael's statement. She politely held out her hand, and the women exchanged awkward greetings.

"She's the goddess, isn't she?" But Christa refused the handshake.

Jenny tried to change the subject. "It's nice to meet you. Your daughter is lovely."

Christa made up a fast excuse and left the office. "I'll meet you at the car, Michael," she said.

When Christa and the baby were gone, Jenny flew at Michael. "She was clearly upset." She stomped her foot. "How could you be so rude and insensitive?"

"What are you talking about? All I did was introduce you." He explained that he had told Christa all about his love for Jenny, and that she understood their marriage was solely for the sake of Lauren. She knew about the cancer. She knew everything.

Jenny was shocked. "I cannot believe you are so cruel to that poor woman."

"You made me live without you. You told me to make a life. Christa got pregnant. What was I supposed to do? I thought you were dead."

Jenny held up her hand to make him stop. "I didn't know I was going to get well. I didn't plan on you finding me."

"I saw your name on one of my checks. The address was right there on your old office. After years of doing business with Alan's Landscaping and your dad, what did you expect?"

She paused for a minute. "So, you still have an account with me?"

He nodded. There was no way to sever all ties with him if they had business with each other.

"Ugh." She was exasperated. "This is impossible."

"You haven't changed a bit," Michael said.

"Neither have you," Jenny chuckled.

Jenny couldn't resist the way he smiled at her.

"So I'll see you later next week?" Michael probed. "We have contracts to flesh out."

"Sure, we do."

When Michael left, she sat on her office chair and took a deep breath.

Over the next few weeks, Michael and Jenny did spend quite a bit of time together in the office and off site at work locations. He even arranged a few new clients for her. They spoke of work and how the weather slowed their projects. No Christa, no baby, no memories. And certainly, no Dr. Scott. On their way home from a dig site, they rode back to the office in her car. He suggested they go somewhere to talk, and Jenny had an idea. The car spun around and stopped in front of the little café they went to that first day they met.

Michael smiled. "All these years later and you still remember."

"I remember everything," she said.

They sat at their old table and reminisced. Michael told her again how he came to marry Christa, but he never stopped loving her, his goddess.

"I understand. You have a daughter to think about." Jenny was a little relieved that he had taken the big step. Then again, he was her Michael, even though he was someone else's husband. She felt hollow inside.

"I can't tell you how happy I am that you're doing so well," he said. He told her about imagining her standing next to him at his wedding, and she laughed.

"We're older and wiser, aren't we," she admitted. "Yes, we still love each other, but with our situations, it's best for everyone if we close the chapter."

Michael moved his chair closer and held her hand. "No." His voice was soft, but held conviction. "I will not accept that. I've lost you too many times. I get to win this time."

Jenny started to cry. "Do you have any idea what it did to me to see you holding your baby? Meeting your wife? You took vows before God,

Michael. I'm not ruining that. There are things we just have to accept...this is our life now."

"Jenny, you know I can't accept that," Michael said, and Jenny believed him. "My feelings haven't changed and I don't think yours have either."

"You have a beautiful daughter and a wife. Don't ruin the life you've built because of me." Jenny desperately pleaded with Michael through fits of tears.

"Actually, I'm about to have a second child, but that's beside the point."

Jenny couldn't believe what she was hearing. He was about to have another child with Christa, but proclaiming his undying love for her. It was bizarre. He would give up everything for her, and that was scary to Jenny.

"I know everything is hard on you just like it's hard on me, but what do you want me to do? I can't live away from you. I want to be with you. I still just want to take you in my arms and show you how much I miss you."

Michael kissed Jenny and awakened her feelings for him.

"We should leave," Jenny said.

A few months passed and Christa gave birth to a baby boy. Jenny had extinguished any and all conversations of reigniting her and Michael's fickle flame, but they worked together more often than they needed to and pretended it was just the push and pull of business. Michael realized Jenny might be dating someone. There were mysterious calls during meetings and times when she was not where she said she was going to be. It had been a long time. He didn't expect her to never date again, and yet he still hoped she would one day come back to him.

A year later, Michael met his staff for a business lunch at a bar and grill by his office. He spotted Jenny on the other end of the bar having lunch with a man he couldn't see. As Michael watched, she laughed and tossed her hair. Jenny reached across and touched the man's hand.

Who was this guy? Michael fumed. His secretary noticed the look on his face and asked him if he was okay.

Michael asked if he could arrange another time for their meeting. Everyone knew by the look on his face that he was angry, so they left.

Michael watched for a bit. He saw the guy stand, lean over and kiss her lips, and walk to the men's room. It was Dr. Scott. Michael walked to the other end of the bar and saw Jenny's startled look.

"So, you and the doctor, huh?"

Jenny's face felt hot. "Michael, don't throw anything."

At that moment, Dr. Scott returned to the table to see a hulking guy confronting Jenny. He recognized the figure as Michael, but before he could get a word in, Michael grabbed his shirt. Jenny begged him to let go, which he eventually did. Unsure of what to do next, Michael resorted to violence, this time, toward a restaurant table, which he flipped emphatically. Dr. Scott cleaned up the mess Michael had left behind as Jenny sobbed in terror.

In his car, Dr. Scott turned to her, "Would you like to explain what the hell that was all about?"

"We dated a long time ago. His temper was part of the reason we broke up. We still have business together. Maybe he was just drunk and lost it."

Dr. Scott shook his head. "I don't understand how he could do that. He has to understand that you have your own life, and he needs to leave you alone." And he sped off.

Michael went to the house he built for Jenny to drink and calm down. He couldn't accept that Jenny was dating someone else. How was it that this guy good enough for her, but Michael wasn't? Confused, he made his way home to his wife and kids. He found Christa sitting on the couch and knitting a blanket for their third child.

Michael grabbed a glass of whiskey and stared at her.

What was he doing with his life and with this woman? "Are you all right?" Christa questioned.

Without hesitation, he lifted her from couch, and they ascended the stairs to a bedroom. Christa wasn't sure how to react. If they weren't making babies, the couple usually wasn't having sex. She let her limbs hang loose as Michael threw her on the bed and began taking his clothes off. When he slammed his body into hers, it hurt. At one point, she screamed. "Stop! What are you doing?" She couldn't believe he was treating her like this.

He snapped out of it and apologized. Kissing her gently, he told her that he had to go take care of something and would be back.

She was so confused and didn't know what to think of her husband. "Where are you going?"

"I don't know. I have some problems, and I'm really sorry, but I have to leave now." He kissed her forehead again and covered her up.

He got in his car and headed straight toward Jenny's apartment, where she lay awake thinking of the altercation at the restaurant. Would Michael ever change?

When Michael arrived at Jenny's door, he knocked several times. Afraid to let him in, she ignored him.

"Jen, I know you're there. Open the fuckin' door."

She yelled back, "Are you going to be crazy if I let you in? I've had enough of your temper for one night."

He spoke quietly. "Just let me in. I wanna talk to you." She unlocked the door and walked away. He walked in slowly with his hands up, signaling safety. Then, his tone got serious. "I've hurt my wife, Jenny. And it's because of you."

Jenny cried, "Michael, what did you do to her?"

"I didn't beat her, geez, I'm not an asshole,"

Michael shouted. "Who do you think I am?" Jenny didn't respond.

"Here, I'll show you what I did to her."

"No, stop it. This isn't a game." Jenny didn't like where this was going. Despite her protests, Michael swooped in and swept her off her feet, throwing her over his shoulder like a sack of potatoes. She kicked and screamed. "Where are you taking me?"

He shifted her into his car and drove in the direction of the house he built for her. They arrived and parked in the driveway. He threw her over his shoulder once more, this time transporting her to the bedroom. He locked the door, and as he took off his clothes, he commanded Jenny to do the same.

She wanted to be furious, but it felt so good, so familiar, that she couldn't bring herself to ask him to stop. "Please don't do something you will regret. You have a wife and kids to think about, and I don't want to be the other woman. This isn't worth it."

"Not worth it. Not worth it?" He was furious now; Jenny had clearly hit a nerve. "Dr. Scott is worth it, but with me, it's not worth it?"

"You have to understand, Michael. We both needed to move on with our lives."

He unbuttoned the front of her blouse. If she wouldn't take her clothes off, he would make her. He kissed, then nibbled, and then bit each breast. Jenny made every effort to resist his advances, but lost all control. Succumbing to the moment, she wrapped her arms around him and dug her nails into his back the ways she used to so many years ago. "How could you be with another guy if you love me?"

Michael said through ragged breaths. "I love you, but I won't be responsible for ruining your life." She was playing with his hair, running her hands through it like sand in a sandbox. He grabbed her blouse and attempted to fully remove it and reveal her torso.

"No. I don't want you to see my body."

"Why not? I've seen it plenty of times before."

There were scars, from surgery, she explained to him. But he had been there through it all. He knew they were there, and he didn't care.

"Let me see you. Let me feel you. I love you, every part of you, no matter how you look."

Jenny gave up the battle and let him take off the rest of her clothes. He saw the scars and gently touched each one, kissing them as he took in every inch of her body.

"I love you, too." Jenny surprised herself when she whispered those four loaded words into Michael's ear.

After an intense evening tangled in each other's arms, Jenny woke to find Michael straightening his tie and buttoning up his slacks. She spotted her torn blouse lying on the ground at his feet.

"How am I going to leave? You shredded my shirt," she teased.

"What makes you think you're leaving?" Michael wasn't joking.

"What do you mean?" Jenny was confused.

Michael finally had Jenny in the house he built for her, and he intended on keeping it that way. He informed her that the doors would be locked, all escape routes blocked, and only he knew the code to set her free. She wouldn't be leaving anytime soon.

"Are you out of your mind?" she yelled.

"I've let you go too many times, and I won't repeat my mistakes." He kissed her cheek and raised his eyebrows, "Just trust me."

He left the room and Jenny followed behind him shouting, "Michael, please wait. You can't leave me here. I have a job, too, you know."

"Call in sick," he said. "I'll be back later tonight."

He's crazy, Jenny thought as she leaned against the wall in the foyer.

Michael would go back to his house where Christa and the kids were usually watching cartoons and eating in the dining room. Christa noticed that he dressed up more often, and he never return home at night.

"We hardly see you anymore," Christa said, pulling Michael aside.

"I've had a lot of business to take care of." He brushed her off.

"What kind of business requires you to stay out so late?" She was beyond skeptical of him, and Michael didn't like to be questioned. "You're acting different, dressing different. What are you up to? Or better yet, *who* are you up to?"

"I've always been honest with you, even when you didn't want to hear it. And so, yeah, I am up to something," Michael confessed. "It's Jenny, I'm seeing her."

Christa cupped her face with her hands and sobbed. Michael knelt down in front of the wicker kitchen chair where she sat, putting his hands on her knees.

"You know I love her, Christa. You've always known. I love you, too, in a different way. But I can't live without Jenny. And of course, I love our kids." He pulled out a handkerchief and wiped her tears. Jenny was his Achilles heel, and his whole world revolved around her happiness and health. "How could you do this to me?" Christa yelled. She didn't see things the same way Michael saw them. "What about our growing family? Don't you want to be involved? Aren't the children more important than Jenny?"

"It's been over twelve years, mine and Jenny's relationship. I just can't kick her out of my life," Michael said. "I love our children, Christa. How could you even question that? I promise you that what I have with Jenny will never interfere with the lives of our children."

"This isn't the marriage I expected," Christa admitted through a stream of tears. "You are sick and need help."

Michael kissed her hand, and Christa pushed him away.

"If you can't live with me anymore, I would understand. I want both of you in my life, but if you can't handle that, then divorce is always an option."

He was giving her an ultimatum.

Jenny spent most of her locked-up hours trying on Michael's shirts and taking hot baths to relax. She was pissed because he forced her into this lifestyle. But she didn't mind curling up next to the fireplace in the living room and watching television on occasion. To pass the time, she would contemplate a strategy for dealing with Michael's craziness.

One day, when he arrived back at the house, Jenny heard the door slam behind him. She turned the volume down. He walked in carrying shopping bags filled with clothes for Jenny. He held them out like a peace treaty. "Are you still made at me?"

Jenny looked at him but didn't say a word. He opened the bags and displayed the new items he'd purchased for her.

"Thanks, but no thanks," Jenny said sourly. "I don't need them."

He looked down at her Metallica shirt. "Well, you are wearing my sleeping shirt, so I think you do need them." He thought he was being funny.

Truthfully, Jenny couldn't help but smile. She was still angry with him, though.

"You realize that what you're doing to me right now is no different than what Richard did, right?"

Michael hated being compared to Richard. He was a scumbag. That line cut deep.

"He locked me in the basement, abused and tortured me to the brink of death, and now you are reminding me of it."

"I'm sorry, it's just, I want you forever," Michael said. "What about your wife and kids?" Jenny wouldn't let it go, and Michael insisted that the arrangement wouldn't affect them.

"I still love them and take care of everything they need, doctor's appointments, groceries, toys, everything."

The kids were one thing, but what about his wife.

Jenny wasn't about to wreck their marriage.

"What have you told your wife?" she asked through pursed lips. "Did you tell her where you've been, where you're going?"

Michael replayed events of that morning and Jenny grew more furious with each new detail.

"How could you do that to that poor woman?"

But Michael didn't get it. In his mind, he was doing her the ultimate favor, telling her the truth unlike those guys who just operate behind their wives' backs. At least she didn't have to wonder what he was up to.

"You don't even know her," Michael added. "Why do you care?"

"I don't have to know her to care," Jenny said. "I only know one thing, and it's that what we are doing is wrong on so many levels."

He disagreed. "Listen, I don't want to come over every day and fight. You are to listen to me and do what I say."

Jenny laughed. "That's hysterical, Michael. When have you ever known me to follow the directions of anyone but myself? You need to stop this madness and let me go."

He stood up and steadied himself with his arm on the wall. "No. Every time I listen to you, you leave. It's not your turn anymore. I want to live my life with you the way I dreamed of thirteen years ago."

He kicked the glass table in front him and it shattered near Jenny's feet. "I don't want to talk about this anymore," he declared, and retreated upstairs to cool down.

A few hours later, he found Jenny asleep on the couch. He picked her up, careful not to wake her, and brought her with him to the bed upstairs. She woke up to him massaging her back and playing with the buttons on her jeans. Like clockwork, they were in each other's arms and making love again. It was just so easy.

As the days passed, Jenny became more frustrated with her imprisonment. The house was nice, sure, but too much of a good thing can quickly turn bad. Her mind diverted to scheming an escape.

Christa decided that she didn't want to leave Michael. Her marriage was important to her, plus, he provided for her in all the ways that mattered. She had a big house, food on the table, and clothes for herself and her kids.

What more could she really ask for?

Dr. Scott visited Jenny's mother after his girlfriend had been missing for about a week. He couldn't get a hold of her and even Sarah didn't know where she was. He drove past her office, but it had been closed since the restaurant debacle, and frankly, Dr. Scott didn't know what to do.

A plan came to Jenny. She grabbed a sharp knife from the kitchen and slid it into the front door latch. This wasn't any old door, however, and it wouldn't unlock.

Then, she punched in random numbers, hoping to magically crack the code and secure her freedom. But nothing worked. She would have to flirt her way out of this.

When Michael got home, he found Jenny sitting by the fire. It had become their routine. "What have you cooked for dinner tonight?"

Jenny shot him a look of disbelief. "Dinner? Do I look like your maid?"

He was teasing her, but Jenny wasn't in the mood for jokes.

"Well, don't you know as the woman of the house, you're supposed to cook dinner, clean, and do the laundry? You live here now, and those are the rules."

Jenny was seriously upset, which she made sure Michael knew by hitting his chest and screaming. "You are absolutely crazy. A mad man!"

He apologized. A small consolation to Jenny who could feel herself getting weaker the longer she was cooped up in the house.

She hadn't taken her medication for days, and the next morning, Michael couldn't wake her up.

He drove her to the emergency room. After Jenny was rushed away by a group of nurses, the doctor approached him.

"What happened to her?" Michael asked.

"Her blood pressure was very low. Her charts show that she should be taking medication to control that, but she must not have been taking it."

"No, she hasn't had it for a few days," Michael said.

He felt bad for what he did to her.

"She's doing fine now," the doctor said. "You can go see her."

In Jenny's room, Michael stared at the IVs and tubes hooked up to her.

"I'm sorry I did this to you. You should've told me you needed your medications." He promised to stop by the pharmacy on their way home, once she was released.

"I don't want to be locked up again. I have a life, Michael. I need to get back to work."

He ignored her. "I'm going to run some errands, check on the wife and kids. Be back soon."

He left the room and Jenny prepared for another round of tests.

Later that night, Jenny reached for the phone on the bed stand. She called Dr. Scott and arranged for him to pick her up immediately. Michael would be back anytime now, and Jenny didn't want to risk being locked up again. Dr. Scott would take Jenny to her mom's house, where she planned to figure out a way out of this whole Michael mess.

When Michael arrived at the hospital and saw no sight of Jenny, he approached the first nurse he could find. "Where is the woman who was in room 3B?"

"Umm, I believe a light-haired man, about this high," she said moving her hand up about a foot above her head, "came to pick her up about an hour ago."

Michael was furious. Frantic, he drove all around town looking for Jenny. He went to her apartment, her office, and finally, to her mom's house.

"Jen, Michael's at the door." Her mom was apprehensive to open it.

"Tell him you don't know where I am," Jenny directed. After that, she could only hear bits and pieces of the conversation from her hiding spot in the downstairs coat closet, but she could tell Michael was upset.

"I'm worried about her and don't know where she is," he said, a little too forcibly for Jenny's mother. "I need to tell her I love her, and that I'm sorry."

"I wish I knew where she was at, son, but you'll be the first to know when I do."

Jenny always appreciated her mom's blunt demeanor. She was sweet as cinnamon rolls, but with a fiery-hot bite like jalapenos.

"He looks pathetic, Jen. Why are you playing these games with him?" her mom asked.

"I love him, mom, but what we are doing is wrong. He has to understand that he can't lock me up to keep me, especially when he has a wife and kids relying on him.

Our circumstances would have to change, and I don't see that happening anytime soon." She cried into her mother's shoulder and they held onto each other tightly.

Michael gripped the steering wheel while the gears turned in his mind. What had the nurse at the hospital told him? Something about a light-haired, tall guy. Then, he remembered. Dr. Scott.

That skeevy Dr. Scott must have given her a ride, so he has to know where she is.

Michael entered Dr. Scott's clinic like a tornado. He didn't bother to consult the woman behind the front desk. Without knocking, he opened the door to the doctor's office and lunged at him, grabbing him by the collar of his shirt, and forcing him to his back on the desk.

"Where is she?" Michael yelled. "Where is Jenny?"

Dr. Scott reached his hand up toward Michael's face and sideswiped him with a devastating right hook.

"Leave now, or I will call the police," Dr. Scott said.

"I dare you," Michael said, as he attempted to regain composure. "I would love to tell them how you kidnapped my wife."

"That's hilarious," Dr. Scott scoffed. "For starters, she isn't your wife, not even close to it. And if anybody is guilty of kidnapping here, it's you."

Michael knew he was right, so he returned to his vehicle defeated and bruised.

After seeing a few more patients, Dr. Scott went to visit Jenny, who was still at her mother's house.

"Michael's getting worse," he told her.

"What do you mean?"

"He came by the office today, held me down. I had to punch him. He called you his wife. He's delusional. It all needs to stop," Dr. Scott said.

"Maybe he's drinking again," Jenny offered instead. If psychology classes had taught her anything, it was that she couldn't dismiss a person as crazy. There was almost always something more, something deeper. But she did agree; this behavior was out of line.

"I just don't really even care anymore," Jenny said. "I'm so exhausted by the situation, and I feel like I've lost myself in the middle of it all." Dr. Scott looked at her with sad eyes.

"I've been thinking a lot, and I think it's time I do something, make a change."

This caught Dr. Scott's attention. "Are you breaking up with me?"

"Yes, and no. I don't know." They both paused. "Look, I need to travel. I need to leave the country and distance myself from everything. The death and pain of the last few years, and both you and Michael..." She was done with men fighting for her affection and building their lives around her. She craved independence and adventure; she had for a long time.

He tried to act like he understood, but Jenny knew he didn't. "You want to leave me. I haven't been good enough to you," he said.

"That's not it at all." She put her hand on top of his. "I need to be happy with myself before I can be happy with anyone else. I'm sorry, I care so much about you, but my heart belongs to Michael. I can't be with him, though, and so it feels like I am in a prison here."

She needed to leave because if she didn't, she would regret it. How could she know if she wanted *forever* with anybody, let alone Michael or Dr. Scott, if she still hadn't seen the things she wanted to see?

"You are a prisoner, but only to your heart," Dr. Scott said.

Maybe he was right, which was all the more reason for her to leave. She stayed with her mother for a few more weeks while she closed the landscaping company and made arrangements for her European escape. Jenny was ready to begin another life, open a new chapter.

A few days before Jenny's flight, a car she had never seen before pulled up and blocked her car in the driveway. Two men in suits got out and went to the front door.

"Are you Jenny Alan?" asked the bigger of the two when Jenny opened the door.

"Yes, may I ask who you are?"

He showed her a badge. "Lieutenant Braque. I'm an investigator from the Oakland County Sheriff's Department."

Jenny invited them in, mystified by what these guys would want with her. The officer sat on the couch and folded his hands.

"We would like to ask you a few questions about your husband, Richard," he said.

Jenny's stomach flipped. "Ex-husband," she corrected. "I sent him divorce papers years ago and haven't heard from him since."

"Can you tell me the last time you saw him?" he asked.

"I think it was about a couple years ago. Why?"

The Lieutenant was aware of Jenny's agitation, but continued his line of questioning. "And why did you file for divorce?"

Jenny cleared her throat. The nightmares had lessened, yet after so many years she still worked to keep Richard from her mind. "You see, he was very abusive. He stole all my money and disappeared. Don't tell me he's come back." Jenny shuddered at the thought. "Would you tell me what's going on?"

"Well ma'am, we've found a body that we believe is Richard. He'd broken out of the Mexican prison he was in, and we found him on the side of the road with this I.D. card on him." The officer showed her Richard's driver's license. "We could really use your help in confirming his identity."

Jenny sat forward. "His body?" She asked. "You want me to identify his body? He's dead?"

"That's right. We just want to show you a picture.

Would you be able to identify him?"

She felt her hands start to shake as she reached for the picture. She looked at the picture of Richard's dead body. He was lying on his stomach, but she could see the brute hands, the sinewy shoulders. There was the tattoo of his family crest on his lower back. All the men in his family had it there. She thought of the rope burns, the assaults, the bread and water. A sense of justice and hope washed over her. This had to be him. She stared for a moment, and the officer broke her frozen gaze. "Are you all right Ms. Alan?" he asked.

Looking into their faces, she handed the picture back. She was all right. "I think that's him.

It's Richard." Although she could only see parts of him, Jenny was sure it was Richard, and she wanted to believe he was gone for good.

"Perez?" The Lieutenant gave the picture to his partner, who wrote on a clipboard and then walked to the corner of the room and phoned the office.

"We had previous evidence of abuse, Ms. Alan. There was a raid, and his gang members testified in exchange for reduced jail time. The D.A. was looking for the leader, who happened to be your ex. They say he rose through the ranks of the Mexican cartel pretty quickly. We've got names, the guy who killed him, and the money— everything we need to put a whole lot of bad guys away for a very long time." Lieutenant Braque seemed pleased to be giving her this news. He knew the stories of Richard's abusive treatment. "Apparently, he really got into bragging to his buddies."

Perez spoke up. "We're all set. We thank you for your help ma'am." He handed her his card, and he left. It was over.

Dr. Scott was heartbroken. Michael continued calling Jenny, unaware that she had recently left for Rome. She'd been living with some cousins on the outskirts of the city and had already met a nice family, who gave her a job and integrated her into their burgeoning social life.

Michael went to see Dr. Scott; he figured the Dr. would have some information about Jenny's whereabouts. When Dr. Scott saw him coming into his clinic, he didn't see the strong, confident guy who'd threatened him a few months before. He motioned to the chair in front of his desk. "Sit," he said.

"Do you know why I'm here?" asked Michael. "I want to apologize for the way I acted before. I wasn't in my right mind."

"Accepted." Dr. Scott nodded.

Michael sat forward and started explaining himself. "Look, I'm not crazy. I know Jenny told you that she and I have been together on and off forever. I'm in love with her, and I'm worried."

"I know, she told me everything." "Where is she?

"She's in Italy. And she's fine," he said.

Michael sat back. "Italy? So she just left?"

Dr. Scott leaned back, too, and clasped his hands behind his head. "Yep…she left us just like that."

Michael asked, "What did she say?"

"The last thing she told me is that she didn't love me. Then she talked about you. She didn't want you to cheat on your wife. She said she deserved a life, and you deserved a family. That's it, man. Sorry."

Tired and sad, Michael sat at home in the dark, drinking and crying. When Christa came to check on him, she found him in bad shape, hovered over the kitchen counter and crying like a young boy. She hadn't seen him this way in a while, but when he was plastered on whiskey, it was usually over Jenny. She got close to him and asked him what the matter was.

"I'm a bad guy, Christa. You've been so patient and kind."

Christa hugged him. "I love you Michael; tell me what's going on."

Michael slurred his words. "She's gone. She's gone for good. I hurt you. I hurt her, and she left so that you could have a better life with me. Jenny did that for you. That's the kind of person she is."

Christa was astonished. From what he'd told her in all his drunken rambling, she thought he said that Jenny left Michael because she wanted him to be with his family.

Should she be upset at his bumbling state or relieved that this woman was out of their lives? She led him to the bedroom and removed the covers so he could lie down. As she helped him take his clothes off, her fingers brushed over his chest.

In his stupor, Michael believed it was Jenny's hands he felt. "Oh, Jenny, your hands feel amazing." He hugged Christa and kissed her neck. "I love you Jenny, please, don't leave me again, ever."

Christa was shocked and sad, but this was the man she had married. So she helped him and hoped he'd forget this moment by the morning.

Michael was depressed beyond description at this point. He couldn't get over the seemingly insurmountable distance between him and Jenny, and he'd been spending hours sitting alone in the house he built for her. Pictures of Jenny adorned the walls. It was like she was staring at him no matter where he walked.

Some afternoons, he would leave the office early and take a nap in their bed, resting his head on the bed sheet where her perfume still lingered. He'd sleep through the night, never returning to his family, to his Christa and the children. But in the morning, he'd be back at the house with a

fake, cheerful disposition and usually making
pancakes.

Chapter Five

etween the monumental, ancient structures and crowded transportation systems, the world seemed so big to Jenny. She didn't quite know where she fit in this new space in this different culture with its foreign foods and language. Although this world looked like heaven, she felt alone. More often than not, she traded in sightseeing and tourist delights for her bed, where she cried, imagining that Michael was in Italy with her. During that first year, Jenny developed a new love, but not for another man.

She'd fallen head over heels for a nearby lake.

Most days, she spent hours sitting on the shore and thinking about Michael. The residents of her apartment building were the only things that kept her from leaping into the frigid waters. Everyone there welcomed her. Her neighbors checked on her regularly, brought her fresh breads from the market, and invited her to lunches and dinners.

For a year, she'd been working in a small family- operated greenhouse with a little flower shop in front. The owners were a married couple expecting their first baby in a few months. Paula took an instant liking to Jenny, and Mark loved having someone to help his wife. There was also Ray, Paula's brother, who helped them maintain the business. Though shy at first, he and Jenny became fast friends. Jenny had been very quiet about her experiences over the past few years. She figured the fewer people who knew about her, the better.

At Paula's baby shower, Jenny couldn't hide her sadness very well.

"Is something bothering you?" Paula asked. "You haven't been your usual cheery self today. I want you to be happy, too."

Jenny hugged her new friend. "I am very happy for you, just dealing with some demons."

Paula wasn't taking that as an answer. And finally, Jenny felt she had to explain. "A few years ago, I found out I had cancer. I had tumors removed from my uterus, and it's not certain that I will ever be able to conceive a baby of my own. It's just a little tough to think about sometimes."

Paula hugged her tight. "Things are so awesome with medicine now, I'm sure there's somebody somewhere that could help you. You can't give up hope."

Jenny wiped her eyes. "Oh, I'm sure of it. But anyway, no worries. Let's go kill that cake."

Motherhood wasn't the only concern. Jenny wasn't too worried at first. Then, what seemed like the flu started to get to her. Her stomach was upset and slightly swollen. She had a feeling of malaise that made her have to drag herself through her days at the flower shop. It had been a while since she'd had any blood tests or even a general exam. Depression and loneliness captured her completely.

It was a cold and foggy day. No one thought it best to be outside. But Jenny found herself alone, sitting on a bench at the lake. She thought about how she had come to Italy to find herself. She laughed. She'd found something, all right. What she'd realized was that time away from those she loved emphasized her feelings for them. From Michael, Oliver, and James to Hanna, Jack, and her father, the pain resurfaced in ways she had never experienced before. A dense patch of fog encircled her, and the temperature seemed to have dropped ten more degrees.

Tears were falling from her eyes when Ray came up behind her with a coat.

"You don't want to freeze out here," Ray said. "What are you doing here?" she asked, surprised to meet anyone on her lake.

"You weren't in your apartment, and Paula sent me to find you."

Jenny wiped her tears with the sleeve of the fleece jacket Ray had given her. He handed her a handkerchief, and she took it gratefully.

"Are you okay?" He didn't want to pry, but she looked helpless.

"I'm fine." Jenny didn't want to get into the story right now.

"It's getting cold and dark," Ray said. "Shall we head back to the apartment?"

Jenny nodded, and together they walked toward home.

When they were about two blocks from her apartment, Jenny felt dizzy and fell to the ground.

Ray carried her to her bed and called Paula and Mark over to help. Paula picked up a bottle of pills from Jenny's bedside table. She hadn't been taking them. Paula got a glass of water and handed it to Jenny, along with one of the pills.

Paula, Ray, and Mark left the room to discuss next steps. They would have to keep a much closer eye on her from now on.

The construction business was competitive, and with rising interest rates, business was slowing.

Michael had become so depressed that he didn't want to go to work or see anyone. His business was losing money, and Christa discovered he'd tried to cover payroll with their savings. There was barely anything left, and she demanded he come up with a solution fast.

Christa found Michael in the den drinking again. "I paid a visit to your parents today. We're trying to figure out a solution to our financial problems, Michael. This is getting serious."

Michael glared up at her, "I don't need you to get involved. It's not your business."

"Michael, I'm trying to help." She told him she was worried about paying bills and taking care of their kids.

Michael stood up and slammed his drink on the table. "Is that what you care about? You afraid of being broke? You had no right to speak to my father about what is going on in my business. You have a home, a car, money, food, and drink. What else do you want?"

Christa screamed back at him, "I want a secure future."

Michael ignored her and walked up to his bedroom. She followed.

"Michael, your father told me that you have a huge house. Why do you have another house?" She waited for his reaction.

"We're not talking about that. It's not your business."

"Your dad said it's worth five million dollars. Where is it? Why do you have this house when our bank account has next to nothing? I have the right to know. I'm your wife."

Michael got into his bed.

Christa tugged at the covers. "Talk to me Michael, I need to know what's going on."

He saw the pain and confusion in her eyes. "All right. Fine." He threw the covers down. "I built that house for Jenny back in 1996 when I met her. It took me two years to finish it. I told you that I love her, and that I had planned to marry her, but then things changed." Michael pulled himself out of bed.

Christa broke down. "You have a house worth five million dollars for Jenny, and I live here in this house with my kids with all the financial struggles?"

"Don't you get enough? You have everything any other woman would dream of."

She cried, and he sat on the floor in front of her.

"Christa, I know that I'm impossible, but I want you to know that I do care about you and I love our kids. I don't know how you've been so patient with me." He put his head in his hands. "But please don't bring up the past or try to compare yourself with Jenny. She's not even around anymore."

Christa's head was spinning. This love of his was worth hanging onto this palace of a house he built for the two of them. She could only imagine how extravagant it was. And even now that Jenny was gone, she called the shots in their marriage. When he was good to her and the kids, was only because he was doing what Jenny would want?

"I know you love her, but I want to understand who I am to you. Why did you marry me? If I had really believed we would never have a real marriage, I would've never agreed to it. I took vows before God, and you know that. And now, look, I'm just stuck. I won't be one of those high society divorcees who collects child support and lives with her parents. It isn't going to happen."

"You know, I wish I hadn't fucked this thing up. You are an amazing woman and a great mom."

Tears welled in Christa's eyes, but she shook her head to will them away. "I always wanted you to be mine alone, to win your heart, just you and me. Michael, even when she's not around, she comes between us."

Michael took her face in his hands and kissed her lips. They moved to the bed and their mutual sadness turned to a craving, passionate release. It seemed to be his way of comforting her. Christa didn't care. It was the attention she longed for.

A few days later, Michael was at his palace drinking and looking at a picture of Jenny. In the middle of talking to her, a ghost, he felt sick and decided to go to Christa and the kids. He got worse while he drove and had difficulty breathing. A mild pain throbbed in his chest. He didn't think much of it until he felt the burning.

As soon as he got into the house, Christa saw that Michael looked sick. He fell to his knees, holding his chest. She called for an ambulance.

The ER doctor came out from the exam room and told her what she was afraid of. "His condition is serious, but you got him here in good time. We're going to keep him in intensive care for the night."

Christa stayed with him all night. If it weren't for Jenny, his business would be thriving, he would love Christa, and he wouldn't have drunk himself into this heart attack.

Over the next few days, Michael got stronger. Even though his heart was recovering, he wasn't responding to anything around him. His parents visited and talked to him, but he stared out the window, expressionless.

Doctors diagnosed depression from the heart attack and told his family that he needed more time. Later, after several consults with the psychologists on staff, he was put on anti-anxiety medication.

Christa was asleep by Michael's bed, still holding his hand, when Michael began to stir. She looked at his eyes when he woke. "Michael, can you hear me?"

Michael imagined hearing Jenny's voice and squeezed her hand. "Jenny, thank God. You came back for me." Christa stood and left the room.

Weeks later, Michael was sent home. The doctors cautioned that he should not be left alone and needed constant care. Slowly, he responded to people and gained strength. Christa was a loving caregiver, and the kids were the best antidepressant their father could have wanted.

Over time, Michael felt more anxious doing nothing at home and was impatient to get back to work. He wasn't able to go back full time, but started with a few hours a day.

Most days, Michael woke up happy to be alive. But others, he wondered what it would be like if he were dead. Would Jenny care? Would she visit his grave?

Slowly, but surely, Michael was picking up the pieces of his business. He hired Clare, a lanky, blond sales representative, to share the workload. Michael had finally returned to his take-charge leadership, but not without noticing how well he and Clare worked together. They developed new advertisements meant to show their competitive advantage. Clare brought a new project on board and showed Michael how it would make millions for the company.

One evening, they stayed late to review and sign papers finalizing the big project. Michael was tired, and honestly, a little bored. This was his least favorite part of closing deals.

Clare noticed his frustration. "We're almost done." She laughed. "Just a few pages left." She licked the tips of her index finger and thumb and flipped the next page.

"I forgot how much work this whole 'running a successful business' thing is."

"You should be happy to sign all of these pages.

Congratulations, hot shot."

"Well, I owe it all to you." He really wouldn't have been able to land this client without her.

"Can I let you in on a little secret of mine?" Clare asked.

"Of course."

"Every time I sign a contract, I celebrate by throwing a party at my house."

"I think that's a good thing," Michael said, thinking her admission was actually kind of cute.

"The party is tonight," she added. "You should come; you'd like it. Dress comfortably. It's a casual thing." She pulled a business card from her purse and scribbled her address on the back, handed it to Michael.

Michael didn't bother to stop home. He knew Christa would have questions, and he wouldn't know how to answer them. So he arrived at Clare's house wearing the same button up and slacks he'd had on at the office.

Clare's house was huge with the modern interior characteristic of the generation below him. His car was the only one in the driveway, and suddenly he became embarrassed. Had he come too early? He rang the doorbell, anyway, and was surprised to see Clare in a red dress with a slit up to her mid-thigh.

"I'm sorry if I'm here early," he said.

She passed him a glass of whiskey. She knew him all too well.

"By the way, you have a beautiful home." "Thanks," Clare said. "It's my dream house. Here, come to the living room." She took him by the wrist and walked until they were by the fireplace. Michael sat on the loveseat while Clare put on a record, Mozart's Serenade No. 13.

For an hour, they talked about their work, their passions, their childhoods. And later, they got into the pool in Clare's backyard. Still, Michael was the only guest to have arrived and he got suspicious. What were her intentions, and where would this night take them?

When they returned inside, Clare gave him a warm bath towel, so he could dry off.

"When do you think the rest of your friends will get here?" He tried to sound casual as he rubbed the towel all over his body.

"No one else is coming," Clare said, as if he should have already known that was the case. She set her glass of wine on the stairway and sashayed toward Michael. She fumbled with the zipper on her dress, taking it halfway off and revealing her breasts. Then, she grabbed his hand and placed it on her right breast. "You deserve pleasure, Michael. You're in the office too much and taking care of the wife, the kids. Take a break, enjoy yourself."

"You don't want to be with me, trust me," he cautioned her.

"I bet we're just as good in bed as we are in the boardroom," she flirted.

He had to admit, this girl was getting to him. "I don't doubt that," he agreed. "But, I'm a very tough guy. I fuck hard. Think you can handle it when it's rough?"

"Try me." Clare was daring. She stood on her tiptoes and shifted her weight onto Michael, kissing his lips with vigor. Her fingers maneuvered his shirt buttons expertly, and she licked his chest until she reached the top of his pants. Soon, that button was unlatched, too, and she put all of him in her mouth.

He groaned. This was certainly pleasure, and he needed it more than he realized.

After a few minutes on her knees, Clare got up. "Let's go to the bedroom."

They took their clothes off simultaneously, and she clasped her arms around his neck and her legs around his torso. He threw her onto the bed and forced himself inside of her, moving back and forth so fast that it took her breath away. She screamed. So this is what Michael meant by "rough," she thought.

Within a few months, Clare had other contracts for Michael, and the company began to turn around. Michael valued Clare's contributions, and they spent more time together in meetings, site visits, business dinners, and parties. Their sexual relationship had no limits, each night more intense than the last.

Christa got more and more annoyed. Michael was a great dad to his kids, but she felt like a houseguest. She was certain that Michael was back on his feet and the business was good because he gave her a new car, and she had more money than she knew what to do with. What had it all been for? Could he and his new associate be having an affair?

Christa hung Michael's clothes while he combed his hair in front of the mirror, getting ready for a business dinner. "Who's going to be at this dinner? Who are you always going off to be with?" she demanded.

Michael laughed. "Trust me. It's business. Do you want another new car? New clothes?"

"I know you're seeing someone," she accused.

Michael paused with the comb lodged partly in his hair.

"Yeah, you're rarely ever home, but when you are, you're drunk. I've seen the tubes of lipstick in your car and the foundation on your shirts. It's Jenny again, isn't it? She's back."

"No," Michael said. "I'm seeing another woman, you're right. But it's not Jenny."

"Michael, you promised it was only me and Jenny.

One woman, I could live with, but two? You destroy me." She threw the rest of his clothes on the ground and crossed her arms.

"I don't know what to say, Christa. Maybe the heart attack changed me. I need to feel alive again, and right now, I can make it through the day without crying over Jenny's picture." He left Christa crying next to the bed on her knees.

When he pulled into the driveway at Clare's house, he wondered what she had in store for him tonight. Once he got inside, she gave him his usual glass of whiskey with her usual sultry smile.

"You look pissed off."

"Don't worry about it," he huffed, slapping her ass.

"I'm glad you're still feeling frisky," she said. "I have a bit of a surprise planned. Cathy?"

Out of the corner of his eye, Michael saw a curvy woman with red hair and the biggest breasts he'd ever seen. Freckles dotted her face like constellations. She wore a strappy dress and high-heeled boots. Michael wasn't complaining, but he didn't understand what was happening.

"What is this?" he asked.

"Cathy is here to give us some extra pleasure. You can think of it as a two-for-one deal."

As Clare explained the situation, Cathy dug a tiny plastic bag with white powder out of her wallet. "I've also got some cocaine to add to the mix," the stranger offered.

"This is all brand new to me," Michael said. "But let's do it." At this point, he would've done anything to get his mind off Jenny and his constant inner turmoil.

Clare and Cathy sat on the shag carpet in front of Michael. As Clare loosened his belt buckle, Cathy prepared a line of cocaine in her palm and beckoned Michael to sniff it.

He obliged, and the high ensued immediately. The sex was amazing. This wasn't love, the kind of thing he had with Jenny, but it was enough.

For the next year, Clare and Michael experimented with new sales tactics and interesting sex positions.

Christa, who accepted her husband's infidelity, satisfied herself with spending the money Michael wasn't dropping on drugs.

"Your keys, sir."

Michael had skipped his lunch hour at work for a visit to the car dealership. He took the keys from the salesman and started the engine of his new sports car. He adjusted the soft leather seat and looked over the gleaming dashboard with its cutting-edge technology. He was taking a drive around the city when his phone rang. It was Clare telling him the final details of a new contract.

"That's exciting," he told her. "Stay there, and I'll pick you up."

Clare was surprised to hear her boss excited about anything. Her surprise turned to shock when she saw him pull up in the shiny new car.

She got in. "Look at you. Is that what you were talking about?"

"Do you like it?" He flipped on his custom sunglasses and peeled out like a teenager, making the tires squeal. The new drugs he was on were lessening the dark clouds. Clare had changed Michael a lot, but deep inside, he still loved and thought about Jenny.

Just when his life seemed to be on the upswing, he got a call one night while lying in bed with Clare and Cathy. It was his mom. His dad had died, and she needed help making the funeral arrangements. Michael's father was the one who'd taught him the value of hard work, who'd given him his first real job at 14, and who'd handed him the keys to his own kingdom soon after.

The loss was hard, and most days and nights following the funeral, Michael could be found lying on the floor of the house he'd built for Jenny, drunk and covered in cocaine.

One evening, Michael left in the middle of dinner with Christa and the kids.

"I'm heading out. I have some things to do."

Christa was mad, but she let him leave without a fuss.

She grabbed her car keys off the counter, loaded up the kids, and followed him. When Michael arrived at Clare's house, Christa watched as two women answered the door. She was furious and swung her car door wide open. It was four women now, and she was ready to end the madness once and for all. She banged on the large, metal doors until Clare finally opened it.

"Give my husband back right now, and don't even think about looking at him again," Christa threatened. "I don't know who you are, but this is over."

Terrified, Clare rushed to Michael's side and urged him out of her home. She was into the fun, not the consequences.

Michael was pissed and two hits into the cocaine, so he was too delirious to understand what was happening.

Clare was too embarrassed to confront Michael about the incident, and she quit without any hard goodbyes.

Michael's marriage grew colder, and his spirits dimmed as he weaned himself off the drugs and alcohol.

Jenny got worse, the longer she was in Italy. She started drinking, sometimes cracking open a bottle of wine at 9 a.m. Ray looked out for her and saw that her condition wasn't improving.

She went to the lake and talked to herself almost every day. For Jenny, the days were empty, sad, and slow. It was close to the last frost, and one evening, she bought a red blend and drank the whole bottle while she perched on her bench near the lake. She crept to the edge, dipped her toes in, and before she knew it, she was neck deep in the icy waters. Her ability to feel anything, physical or emotional, faded and she was happy for the first time in a long time.

She was also dying.

Ray had seen her go in and sprinted toward her. He flung his jacket into the weeds and dove into the water to retrieve Jenny, who was unconscious and barely floating. He got her to land and attempted to drain the water from her lungs. It took ten minutes of CPR to revive her, but she opened her eyes and vomited on his jacket, which was lying beside her head.

Jenny could've sworn the man hovering over her was Michael, but after a few rapid blinks, she saw Ray. He draped his sweater over her, taking the dirty jacket for himself. He hauled her to her apartment and helped her into her bed.

"I can't save you forever, Jenny." Ray was serious.

Her stunt had scared him. "Why do you keep putting yourself in danger?"

"I wish I had an explanation, but I don't know what's going on with me." Jenny was as frightened as he was.

She didn't know her own limits. She feared she would hurt herself past the point of saving, soon, if something in her life didn't change.

"Does it have to do with Michael?"

Jenny was confused by his question. "How do you know about Michael?"

"You call his name a lot, especially while you sleep," Ray said.

She sighed.

"Do you love him?" he asked.

"Do I love him? Ray, he is my whole world. Where he ends, I begin."

"Why don't you just call him?" Ray may have grown up in the country of romance, but he didn't get the concept of forbidden love. Take what you want and hold it tight; that was his motto.

"It isn't that simple," she said. "He's married and has kids. I don't want to ruin his life. You can't let me go back to him, Ray."

"I won't," he promised, and he pulled the covers up, brushed the hair away from her eyes, and closed the door to her bedroom.

Jenny fell asleep to thoughts of Michael. Where was he now? What he was up to? Did he miss her as much as she missed him? A big part of her hoped so.

Chapter Six

Clare had moved on and was now working for another construction company in Lansing. Although she was far away, she still referred clients to Michael. He missed the distraction. It was sweet and filling, like a jelly doughnut. With an endless supply of those around, Michael hadn't thought of Jenny for years. But now that Clare was gone, he returned to his old habits and frequently found himself staring into an empty bottle and Jenny's photo. Christa and Michael barely spoke unless it was about the kids.

Ben needed a new toothbrush. Lauren had a form from school that she needed signed by Friday. It was strictly business between the two of them.

Jenny's illness worsened, and she experienced symptoms that indicated the cancer might have returned. Now an ocean away from Dr. Scott, she was scared and unsure how to handle her situation abroad. Paula and Mark decided it would be best to take her to see one of their friends, a doctor with an office on the Via Frattina.

With her medical history, the doctor believed she was developing a small tumor on her left breast. He recommended surgery and more rounds of chemotherapy. She was devastated. When would it all end?

Back at her apartment, Jenny buried her face into a pillow and cried. Her crying made Ray cry. He would've done anything to help her. Even though she made him promise to leave Michael out of things, Ray found Michael's number in Jenny's phone. He left the room to make the call. When Michael answered, Ray explained who he was and how Jenny's condition had escalated over the past few months. She needed to hear a familiar voice.

"Yeah, absolutely," Michael said. "Put her on the phone."

Ray went back into the bedroom, put his hand on Jenny's back, and gave her the phone.

"What's this?" she asked.

"Michael's on the line," Ray said. "Talk to him, you'll feel better."

"Hello? Michael, is it you?"

"Jenny, my darling, my goddess, Jenny," Michael whispered into the phone. "Are you okay?"

"Michael, I don't want to die here, alone." She sobbed. "I'm sick again, and they say I need surgery."

"I'll book you a flight right now," he said. "I'll take you to Dr. Scott, and you'll be fine. Come back to me, babe."

She agreed to the plan, relieved to have a steady course of action. The two of them spoke for hours—until the lights across Rome dimmed, making way for the stars.

A few days later, Jenny towed her travel bags and delivered heartfelt goodbyes to Paula, Mark, and Ray. She was grateful for their hospitality and friendship, and she vowed to visit them again soon.

Michael, ever the gentleman, had booked her a first-class ticket so she could receive special care during the flight. When Jenny exited baggage claim and met Michael in the airport parking lot, it was as if nothing had changed. They embraced each other with passion, and Michael kissed all over her face.

"Oh, I've missed you, baby," he said. "I love you."

"I love you, too," Jenny said. And this time, she knew she really meant it. They returned home.

As he carried her to their bed as he'd done so many times before, she thought that she might be ready to die there. To stay in his arms, in their bed, until she took her last breath, whenever that may be.

Michael put her in bed and lay next to her. They faced each other in their vulnerability.

"I knew you would come back to me," Michael told her. He was happy to have her around again, but not under these circumstances. "Tomorrow, we'll see the doctor."

Dr. Scott went to meet with Jenny and Michael the next morning. She was lying in a hospital bed asleep, still tired from the long flight the day before. When she opened her eyes, she saw Dr. Scott, who smiled through his tears. He was excited to see her after all this time.

"I'm sorry about leaving you the way I did," Jenny said.

"No, no apologies from you," he said. "It turned out for the best anyway. I'm married now, Jenny, look." He pointed to his ring finger. There was a simple, silver band.

Jenny was happy for him.

My wife and I have a beautiful baby girl. She's spunky already, sort of like you. I'd love for you to meet her one of these days." He gushed. "But, for now, we need to run some tests and figure out next steps.”

After a few rounds of tests, Dr. Scott determined that a biopsy was in order.
Eventually, the lab results revealed that the tumor was benign. All her blood tests came back normal, and she only needed vitamins and regular checkups to monitor her condition.

“You’re weak, that’s for sure, but it’s more of a mental exhaustion. Spend some time with family and friends, and slow down a bit. Enjoy life.”

A lot had changed while Jenny was in Italy. Sarah had moved to Ann Arbor, and Jenny took Dr. Scott’s advice and met her best friend on her new stomping grounds.

“I am more than okay, especially now that you’re here.” Jenny said.

“Let’s go get a drink and dinner. I know a bar and grill around the corner,” Sarah suggested.

They pulled two tall chairs up to the rustic bar, and the bartender told them he knew just what they would like.

Jenny listened while Sarah talked about the man she was dating and that she was going back to college. “He’s just a friend, but we have so much in common," she said. "So, enough about me. Spill. What are you doing in Ann Arbor?"

Jenny told Sarah about Italy. She described the Trevi Fountain and the crowds of tourists with their digital cameras and practical tennis shoes. Jenny talked about nights in romantic Italian eateries with glasses of wine and soothing music. Her trip had been a blast, despite the loneliness. But when she got around to answering Sarah's real question, why she was here, she sighed.

"I'm here because of Michael," Jenny admitted.

And to Jenny's surprise, Sarah was happy for her. "I hope you two end up together for real," Sarah said. "I've known you since the beginning, and you guys are meant to be together."

Jenny wanted to talk about memories of the two of them singing with Oliver, but decided against it. She told Sarah that she missed managing her dad's business. It felt good to let loose of the life-and-death issues and all the ways she had kept secrets from so many loved ones in her life. The only topic she avoided was Richard. For some reason, she couldn't bring herself to unleash those demons. She always felt like he was with her. Even sitting in the bar, she felt a pair of eyes on her, but looked around the room and saw no one.

"Here you are, dears." With a dramatic flourish, the bartender set down two delicate red frosty drinks. "A little citrus and, of course, tart Michigan cherry juice."

Sarah noticed his accent. "You're not from around here, are you?"

"No. this is just my side gig. I'm here with the theater for summer stock. But the performances won't start for a few weeks yet. We're in rehearsals, and the play only runs on weekends, so here I am. It's stellar, dears. You should really come see. It's called *Escanaba in da Moonlight.*"

"Put those on my tab." Jenny heard the gravelly voice beside her and looked up. Her breath caught at the sight of the tall man in a plaid shirt, who stood next to her.

Jenny was terrified. "No. Leave us alone. Back off. Please go away."

The bartender had a few words with the man, who then left for the other end of the bar.

"Were you afraid or something?" Sarah asked. "This is not the Jenny I know. You're much stronger than that."

"I can't help it," Jenny said, out of breath as if she'd been full out running. "Between the cancer scares and depression, I've been a little out of whack."

"I can't figure out why you kept the cancer from me all this time. You need more than just your best friend to talk to, Jen. You need to get professional help."

Jenny sipped her drink. "I've thought about joining a cancer-support group, but Michael never lets me feel down; he always makes me happy. I'm just upset that I'm taking him away from his wife and kids."

"I don't know what to tell you about that, but I do care about you. It's great to see you doing so well."

Jenny eyed the man in the plaid shirt at the other end of the bar and shuddered. He probably thought she was crazy. The bartender brought them a steaming plate of fragrant Mexican food to share. "If anything will make you feel better, it's nachos." He winked.

Jenny spent the next few days with Sarah. Michael was happy that Jenny was not just catching up with her mother, but that she was also

reconnecting with her best friend. She was getting the support that she needed. Sarah and Jenny walked the beach where they used to swim, and they reminisced about how simple their lives used to be.

They even sneaked in to watch a rehearsal of the bartender's *Escanaba* play. She was feeling better than she had in weeks.

"This has been so great spending time together," Sarah said. "I'm glad you're seeing your mother and that Michael is taking care of you, too."

Jenny told her how different she felt from the high school girl she used to be. "I used to wonder if a guy was only interested in me for the way I looked," she confessed. "Now I wonder how Michael could still want me when I'm not a whole, complete woman anymore."

"Jenny, you're still as beautiful as ever," Sarah said.

"I know you're lying, and I love you for it." Jenny hugged her friend. "But going through everything and coming up here, I guess I'm beginning to see what's really important."

It was a Wednesday in early spring, which, in Michigan, means it was still cold and rainy. Jenny went to see her mother while was in town running errands.

"My beloved daughter." Her mother greeted her with a hug. They spent the evening by the fireplace in the family room, visiting and catching up with cups of hot tea. It was a rough adjustment, but Jenny could tell her mom was getting used to her new life. She'd been alone when Jenny was abroad. Now that Jenny was back, she made a point to stop by as often as she could.

"I know you've only been back for a few weeks, but it feels so good to have you here." She hugged her daughter.

"I won't leave. I'll stay, and we will always see each other," Jenny said.

It had been a long time since Jenny had gotten to feel like a little girl. She was able to put aside her fears for just a little while.

Within a year, Jenny regained her strength. She and Michael sat in the waiting room at Dr. Scott's clinic. A few minutes later, he walked over to them with a huge smile on his face.

"Jenny, I think we can lessen the frequency of our visits. You are in the clear and have been for a while now."

Jenny and Michael were still beaming when they got to the car. They got to the house, and Michael picked Jenny up, and they ascended the stairway to the bedroom. As he lowered her onto the bed, Jenny said, "Michael, we need to talk." Michael froze.

"You've been spending too much time with me since I got back. I'm taking you from your family, your kids. I feel bad for what this is probably doing to Christa. Doesn't she wonder where you are?"

"I did horrible things to Christa while you were gone, Jenny. And our relationship isn't going to bounce back from that damage. I might as well tell you now. I had an affair with a co-worker, and Christa found out. I'm a terrible person, and I get it if you want to leave."

Jenny was shocked, but she understood. He'd never been happy with Christa. It was more of an imprisonment with a life sentence than a marriage.

"You aren't as terrible as you believe," Jenny said. "You've spent your life trying to get your mind off of me, and for that, I am so sorry."

He didn't like when she apologized for his response to pain, but still, he appreciated the gesture.

Then, Jenny turned serious. "You do need to manage your time better, though. Choose your kids over me as often as you can; that's all I ask."

"That's fair," he said, and prevented her from saying another word by leaning in for a long, slow kiss.

"We are crazy," Jenny shouted.

"Crazy in love," Michael said, and they moved in unison underneath the sheets.

The next morning, sunshine glimmered through the windows. Jenny wanted to look as good as the warmth felt on her face as she lay in bed. She put on a floral romper and headed to the nearest salon. She got her hair cut and her nails painted. For the first time since she was diagnosed with cancer, she felt like the beautiful goddess Michael always claimed she was.

Michael stopped by Christa's house after work, where the kids were sipping from juice boxes and coloring. He took a crayon and drew a turtle next to Ben's sand castle in the beach scene he was creating.

Christa noticed a change in Michael. "You're a happy camper today," she commented, her tone snarky. "What's different?"

"Just having a good time with the kids, Christa." He didn't want to get into this with her today, but he had a feeling the topic of Jenny couldn't be avoided.

"I just haven't seen you this happy in a while," she said.

"Let's talk about this later, when we're alone."

Later that afternoon, Michael was polishing his shoes and getting ready to leave when Christa took a seat on the bed. She watched him tie his shoelaces and check himself in the mirror. "Please, tell me what's going on. Is it another woman?"

"Not another woman," Michael replied, cryptically. "There's only one. Jenny is back."

She leaned her body against the vanity. "That explains everything. The late nights, the text messages and phone calls. Of course it's Jenny again. Who else would it be?"

Michael could tell that Christa was tired of playing second fiddle. "I wanted to keep it from you because I knew her return would hurt you." Michael tried to reason with her.

"Why do you love her so much, yet still keep me around? How have you two not drifted apart after all these years?" She was angry.

Michael put his hands on her shoulders. "I'm sorry, Christa. I've been a terrible husband to you. And while I wish I could answer your question, even I don't know the answer. All I know is that I've been madly in love with this girl since the day I met her."

Christa shuddered, pushing his hands away. "You've never loved me. Even the kids couldn't make you love me."

"I care about you, and I love our kids. The love I have for you is different than the love I have for Jenny. You are my wife, and you have my name. She doesn't have that."

"She has the only thing that matters," Christa said. "She has your heart."

Lauren squealed in the next room, and Christa left to check on her. Michael hated to leave in the middle of an argument, but Jenny was waiting for him.

In the evening, he went to his and Jenny's house, but Jenny was nowhere to be found. He heard footsteps upstairs and called out to her. "Jenny, I'm home."

As she descended the staircase, Michael caught his breath at the sight of her in a little black dress. Something was different. Had she gotten her hair done? She'd dyed it black, and to Michael, she was perfect. Her beauty sent him straight to his knees, and he kissed her hand as she massaged his head.

"I am the luckiest man in the world," he said. "You are my goddess."

He stood, and Jenny kissed him on the cheek. "Hey, Mr. Lucky Man."

"You look so amazing, and here I am, an old man with wrinkles. I probably smell bad, too."

"Well, don't forget about the gray hairs, too. You are pretty atrocious, aren't you?" Jenny giggled. She missed their banter.

For weeks, Christa let the news of Jenny's return boil like a pot of chili. Soon enough, she was running on a gallon of anger and looking into real estate records, until she found the house that Michael had built for Jenny. She would've just followed Michael, but she wanted to talk with Jenny alone. This was between them, not Michael.

She parked on the side of the street. Christa wanted to see the palace and the princess that lived inside its ornate walls. Her fist pummeled the door as if it were making contact with Jenny's face. *Bang,   bang, bang.*

Jenny opened the door and found Christa in her rough state. From the sight of Michael's wife, Jenny knew this conversation would not end well.

Christa didn't recognize Jenny. She looked more beautiful than Christa had ever imagined. "May I come in?" she choked.

Jenny had decided a long time ago that she owed Christa an explanation of some kind. She just didn't think the time for her to give it would come so soon or in this way. So she let the woman, and the parade of kids she and Michael had produced, into the foyer.

Christa stared above her at the glistening chandelier. It must have been made from Baccarat crystal. As she fumed over the intricacy of it all— the chandelier, the house, Jenny—she hoped her mouth wasn't gaping as wide as she felt like it was.

"You don't look a day over 22," Christa said to Jenny. "In fact, you look younger than the last time I saw you.

How many years has it been?"

"At least 10 years, but probably more," Jenny replied, ignoring the condescension that laced Christa's every word.

"Well, it's no wonder why Michael calls you a goddess.

He's certainly set you up pretty nicely here, hasn't he?"

"I suppose he has."

"Do you even know how much this house is worth? I've seen the paperwork, read the records. You're living in a $5 million home."

Christa's pestering quickly annoyed Jenny. "What can I do for you, Christa? Why did you come here?"

"Sorry, love. I came to see you and the house. I wanted to check that my husband is meeting all of your needs, physical and otherwise."

Jenny didn't appreciate what Christa was insinuating.

But she understood her response and so let her dig in.

"I heard you were in Europe. Why come back? Michael mentioned that you'd made the whole move for me, so Michael would tend to his family." Her tone was accusatory.

"I became terribly ill. I had no choice but to come back," Jenny explained.

"Right now, you don't look like you've been sick a second in your life," Christa said. "I'm impressed."

Jenny knew Christa was mocking her, but she took the bait and quipped back, "Please, call my doctor. Check my medical charts. I dare you. You can ask him about the dozens of rounds of chemotherapy."

"Geez, Jenny. Calm down. I believe you, all right?" Christa said. "I watched Michael cry over you enough times to know the truth."

"Cancer isn't something to joke about, Christa. I know you dislike me, but don't dismiss the disease ever again." Jenny hoped her stern voice would help her point hit home with Christa, and she'd settle down. She escalated.

"Tell me this, then," she started. "Why do you keep pulling Michael around on a string? You love him, and then you leave. You love him, and then you leave. Over and over again, and I pick up the pieces every single time. You're beautiful, clearly. It makes sense that Michael would be crushed over you. But why do you play with him this way? Why can't you just leave our family be?"

Jenny grew tired of the blame game Christa was playing, the pity party she was throwing for herself in the middle of Jenny's hallway.

"What do you want from me, Christa? You've seen me; you've seen where I live. I think that's enough for today."

Christa went for the jugular. She mentioned the value of Jenny's home and kept calling it a palace.

Jenny looked away as she spoke. Finally, she said, "This is not my home. Michael owns this home, just like he owns the home you live in with your kids. I know for a fact that he cares very much for you and for the children. I know he gives you everything you could ever want or need."

Christa considered Jenny's words and shot an evil glare in her direction. "Hmm, Michael is a good father," she conceded, "but he's a terrible husband."

"He isn't a terrible husband," Jenny replied. "He just has the heart of a young boy."

"Wow, that's a great way to put it actually." Christa was shocked and upset. "You know Michael very well, don't you?"

Jenny blinked slowly, and looked straight into Christa's eyes. "I've known Michael for more than 20 years. I know him better than I know myself. I love him more than life itself, and I always will."

"You love Michael, huh? Take him. He's all yours," Christa said. "Our marriage is a sham anyway. It's a picture in a frame. Michael doesn't touch me. We sleep in separate bedrooms." Christa gathered her children and ushered them back through the door of the palace she hated so much. Just like that, Jenny was by herself, replaying the exchange with Christa in her mind until she was sick to her stomach.

It was afternoon, and Michael headed home to see his kids like he always did. When he walked through the door, he saw Christa with a stiff drink in her hand and tears flowing down her face.

When he closed the door, he triggered something inside his wife. She strode toward him with closed fists and beat his chest.

He gently grabbed her wrists, which sent her to her knees.

"What's going on?" Michael asked.

Christa couldn't articulate her thoughts. "You... you... you," she screamed.

He'd never seen Christa behave this way before. Sure, he'd upset her many times during the course of their marriage, but this was different.

"Why do you do this to me? Why did you even marry me? Why did you keep having kids with me?"

"Where is all of this coming from?" Michael demanded.

"I visited Jenny today. At the house you built for her. Or, the palace, I should say."

"Why did you go there?"

"I wanted to solve the mystery. I wanted to understand why you love her so much and me so little. She told me she loves you and she wants you. That's why you give her everything—not just the fancy clothes, cars, and homes— but your heart, too."

Michael wrapped his arms around Christa, helping her off the floor. He led her to the bedroom and insisted that she lay in bed and stop drinking.

"You hate me," she said.

"I don't hate you," Michael said. And he left her there, crying on the bed and alone.

"She's sick, you know? You are both sick," Christa shouted from the bedroom.

Michael went to Jenny's house and found her sitting quietly in the living room. She stared at the television set, but he could tell she wasn't really watching the show. He kissed her hand and sat beside her.

"Are you all right? Christa told me she stopped by. I'm so sorry she did that."

"I was so honest with her. It was probably too cruel," Jenny said.

"She's known for years about our love for each other," Michael reasoned with her. "What really pisses Christa off the most is that she isn't living in this house with its grandeur. She's comparing her situation to yours."

"Go back to her, Michael. She needs you more than I do."

"What I need is you. I need to put my head right there." He pointed to her lap. "And snuggle there like a little boy."

Jenny's eyes filled with tears, and she smiled at him. There was that heart of a young boy. She cherished it so much.

"I don't know what will happen with us, but I can't live without you," she said.

Chapter Seven

Michael, Christa, and the kids sat silently around the kitchen table. They chomped on grilled-cheese sandwiches and slurped tomato soup. As Michael cut his youngest son's grilled cheese into tiny, bite-sized pieces and tickled Lauren and Ben, Christa watched with disdain. It was getting harder and harder for her to separate the husband from the dad. She had been doing it for years, but she couldn't put up the façade any longer, not since Jenny professed her love for Michael to Christa, in person.

Christa motioned to the nanny. "Take the kids outside, please."

Michael took a bite. He looked up from his plate, and Christa had her gaze locked securely on him.

He smiled. "It seems like you want to say something. What do you need? More money?"

"You know what, Michael. No. I don't actually want anything else from you. I want a divorce."

He stopped chewing. "Why would you want that?"

"Do you really even have to ask?" She was irritated by his complete lack of self-awareness. "I've had enough. I'm done being a part of this weird love triangle. I thought things would change after Jenny left, after Clare left, but they didn't. And I don't believe they ever will."

"I know I've been terrible. A divorce is a bit of an overreaction though, don't you think?" As in love as Michael was with Jenny, he wasn't ready to burn down the life he'd built with Christa. It had an odd familiarity to him. If Jenny left, at least Christa and the kids would always be there. Now, that certainty faded away.

"This will make you happier than I ever could. You will be able to marry your goddess." In her mind, Christa had already cut the ties. She was halfway out the door.

"What about the kids?" Michael asked, a tear formulating in his left eye.

"We'll work it out," she said. "You'll see them often. Don't worry."

A week later, Michael and his attorney met to arrange the paperwork. He was really getting divorced from Christa. It was bittersweet, and Michael wasn't sure how to react to the events that unfolded before him. According to the agreement, the pair would share custody of the kids, and all of their belongings would be split 50/50. No hard goodbyes. No hard feelings. The process was fairly quick and painless, all things considered.

When they walked out of the courtroom on the final day of their union, they shuffled their feet in front of the entrance. Michael reached out to Christa with a tenderness he'd never used with her. He kissed her forehead, and they hugged for the last time as husband and wife. Then, he bent down and gave the kids a big bear hug, and they giggled with delight. They didn't know the gravity of the situation they were in, and today, that was okay.

"I'll see you guys tomorrow," he said to his little ones. And he headed toward his car, which he would drive to an unsuspecting Jenny. She didn't need to know about the divorce. He was content with the decision to keep it secret, at least for a little while. There was no need to start a fight now—when he could prepare for it later.

Over the next few months, Michael and Jenny spent nearly every waking moment together. A matinee here, a round of mini-golf there. They were having fun. It felt like they were in the honeymoon stage of their relationship, even though they had known each other for ages. Although Jenny enjoyed his persistent presence, she noticed that she was getting a lot more of him than usual.

From new cars to regular date days and nights, it seemed like she was the only person in his life. What about Christa and the kids? One night over dinner, Jenny decided she'd get to the bottom of this mystery.

"So, how are the kids doing?" she asked with nonchalance. "Are you spending much time with them?"

"I see them every day. They're fine." Michael tried to keep calm, but he knew what Jenny was getting at, and he wasn't in the mood to go there.

"How long do you see them each day? Like, an hour? It's just that we've been going out a lot and having fun, and trust me, I love it. But I don't want to take time from the kids." She thought she was doing a good job. She didn't sound too accusatory. "So what's the deal?" "Nothing."

He thought his short response would fend off her attack.

Jenny only grew more fervent. She felt that he was hiding something from her.

Later that evening, they began making out beneath the covers of their bed.

"I think about you while I'm signing checks and making business calls at work." He was like a schoolboy. "Do you miss me when I'm not around?"

"You're here so much, how could I miss you?" Jenny joked.

Michael laughed. "I love you, Jenny. I can't wait to marry you. Let's go down to the courthouse tomorrow." He was so sure of his idea, and then he realized that Jenny still believed he was married.

"I mean, let's go sometime." His attempt at backpedaling backfired.

"What do you mean? Michael, what's going on? You're not telling me something." Jenny got out of bed, furious.

"It was a mistake. My words slipped. You know I've thought about marrying you since we met. It's constantly on my mind. Nothing more than that."

Jenny let it slide, but something didn't feel right.

Days passed, and Michael spent an afternoon binging a new Netflix show with Jenny. The family in the show was vacationing in Bora Bora.

"We should go," he said to Jenny. "Go where? The store?"

"No, we should go to Bora Bora. Stay in a cabana by the ocean for a couple of weeks. Just you and me, maybe a few margaritas." He smirked, and Jenny thought for a second how charming this man beside her was.

"A couple of weeks?" Jenny shrieked.

"That's seriously all you heard?" Michael asked. "But yes, a couple of weeks. Maybe longer. As long as you want, we can stay."

"And what will Christa and the kids think?" Jenny was shocked to hear this plan come out of Michael's mouth. "You should take them on that trip, not me."

"Jenny, I can do whatever I want. I'm not a prisoner to my life. Stop bringing Christa and the kids up anytime I say any little thing."

It was as if he was spewing fire at her. He went to the liquor cabinet and poured himself a glass of whiskey. As he took a sip, Jenny walked toward him.

"How can you yell at me like this?" she asked.

"I've been spending loads of time with you. All I ask is that you don't bombard me about Christa and the kids during our time together. Is that really so much to ask?"

The next day, Jenny escaped the house while Michael was at work. This time, she would confront Christa on her turf. She had to know what was going on, and Michael hadn't convinced her that it was nothing.

Christa was surprised to see Jenny on her doorstep.

She offered her tea and a seat inside. Jenny noticed a change in her demeanor. Christa looked free, but bitter. Hopeful, but grieving.

"No thank you, that's quite all right. I just came to ask you a quick question," Jenny replied. "This is probably out of place, but my gut is begging me to ask. Is there something going on between you and Michael?"

"Oh, something going on between us? No, no. In fact, I thought you two would have been married by now," Christa commented.

"What are you talking about?" Jenny's jaw stiffened. "How could we be married when you are still together?"

Christa connected the dots. Michael hadn't told Jenny about the divorce.

"Hun, Michael and I divorced over nine months ago."

Jenny started hyperventilating. Her heartbeat ran a hundred miles an hour. She sprinted toward her car. She put the key in the ignition and formulated a plan. How would she bring this up to Michael?

After work that evening, Michael bent down to kiss Jenny. She pushed him away hard and fast.

"What the fuck was that for?" Michael shouted.

Jenny chose to fight fire with fire. She wasn't going to be nice about this breach of trust.

"Did you think you could keep the divorce from me for the rest of our lives? What were you thinking?" Her arms flung over her head in exasperation.

"I'm sorry." Those were the only words he could muster.

"I knew something was going on. You were here too often, bringing new furniture and plates over. I should have known better." Jenny hit her forehead with the palm of her hand.

"Let me come clean," Michael pleaded with her. "It's true. Christa and I divorced. But I get to see the kids every day. I didn't lie about that. I cover their expenses like normal and have shared custody, so they can come over whenever they like."

"Then why haven't they come over?" Jenny threw him a curveball.

"Because, I wasn't ready to tell you. I was scared you would leave me. I didn't ask for the divorce, Jenny. She did."

"Of course, she did. Look at the hell you've put her through. If I were her, I would have left a long time ago."

"It's been 10 months," Michael said. "We've both healed and are moving on. I think you should accept it and be happy."

Jenny covered her face with a pillow and cried. "It's all my fault," she muttered.

"Jenny, you aren't the reason the divorce happened. It was a long time coming; you know that. I married her because I got her pregnant. It was the right thing to do at the time, but we were different people who only grew even more different over time. We would have never worked."

"Leave me alone." Jenny spoke precision.

For the next several days, Michael followed Jenny around the house like a puppy. She wasn't speaking to him. She communicated with him through pointing and eye rolls. Jenny thought it was funny and enjoyed messing with him. After the blowout about the divorce, she had done some thinking. Michael was right, and Jenny needed to put the whole situation into perspective.

Her silent treatment was a game, and she relished the punishment she was doling out to him. It felt like high school all over again. Him, chasing her in his fancy sports car. Her, resisting him at every turn.

Michael grew weary with the back and forth. So one night, he came home carrying a thick file. Jenny was making lasagna and uncorking a bottle of wine for the two of them. She had planned to break her silence over Italian food.

After they began to dig into their pasta, Michael rose from his chair and got down on his knees. Kissing her hand, he said, "I want you to have this." He handed her the file.

"What is this?" Jenny asked.

"Paperwork on the house. I transferred full ownership to you. It's under your name now."

Jenny's eyes lit up. "Why did you do this?"

"I built it for you, and I want you to feel like it's a part of you, too. For it to be a part of you, it has to be yours. I want you to have it. This is your house. You are my lady."

"Be honest. Did you do this so I would talk to you again?" She batted her eyelashes at him.

"Yes and no." He chuckled.

"Let's eat," she said. Her heart was full, but her belly was not.

At the end of the meal, Michael looked at Jenny from across the table. He was mildly intoxicated. It didn't matter though. The words came out like thunder. "Let's get married, for real."

Jenny ignored him and started telling him a joke her dad used to say all the time. One thing led to another and the lovers found themselves in the bedroom.

"You haven't responded to me. I asked you to marry me earlier. Remember?" he reminded her. "This isn't the time or place to ask a question like that." Jenny turned over on her side and shut her eyes.

"Where should I do it, then?" He couldn't understand what this woman wanted from him.

"I don't know," Jenny replied, half asleep already.

Michael turned away from her, pissed that she wouldn't give him a hint.

For days, Michael pondered. He wondered how he should do it. How should he ask his beautiful goddess to marry him? Well, he knew how she loved games. So, he started there. As the days turned into weeks, Michael gave Jenny the silent treatment. They still smiled at each other and went about their normal couple activities. But no words passed between the two of them.

Jenny didn't mind. She caught on to his game, and exactly as Michael had predicted, she couldn't get enough of it. A worthy opponent his woman was.

New Year's Eve was just around the corner, and Michael wanted to celebrate his first year with Jenny— really *with* her—by doing something special. He told her to wear an evening gown and get in the car. They were going to Ann Arbor for the evening. When they arrived in the city, they pulled into the parking lot of The Earle.

Michael ordered an escargot appetizer and top shelf wine. They dined on sautéed duck breasts. It was an extravagant affair.

"What would you think if I said you'd look good in a long white dress right now?" Michael said between bites. "Oh Michael, not this again." Jenny sighed and rolled her eyes. "I love you, but..."

"But, what?"

"You scare me, Michael. I know you. You're the type of guy who is used to getting what he wants, even if you have to force the issue. Then, when you get bored, you move on and find another toy." "You think I will drop you? Just let you go? Never, Jenny. Not you." He tried to assure her. "You're just afraid to commit something real."

"Maybe," Jenny agreed. "I'm afraid I will invest my whole heart into you and then you will change. You will divorce me like you did with Christa."

"Why must we dissect my relationship with Christa all of the time? It's not even remotely similar to what I have with you. It was a marriage of convenience, nothing more."

"So you can promise me that you won't get tired of me? You won't stop loving me and have an affair with another woman?"

"Jenny, I only have eyes for you," Michael said simply. "We've let people, places, and things keep us apart for far too long. From Christa and

Richard to cancer and Europe, we've wasted our years. I don't want to do that anymore."

"Let's talk about this at home," Jenny conceded. "I want to enjoy this meal and romantic setting with you." She gave him a sweet smile, and they continued slicing slivers of duck.

Just as Jenny thought the meal was over, and they were waiting for the check, the waitress came over, along with two cooks, carrying a dish of Baked Alaska. She looked at them, then she looked at Michael, who by this point, was on one knee beside her with a velvet box.

He cracked it open, and the ring inside glimmered.

Jenny shook her head, and her face got red. She picked up the ring, inspected it, and then set it on the table with a shrug.

"What's that about?" Michael questioned. His eyes darted back and forth. "People are staring. Aren't you going to answer?"

"Nope." Jenny chuckled. "You think proposing to me in public means you'll get an automatic 'yes' out of me? You're a rookie if you think that." She was messing with him, and it was even more fun now than when they were at the house.

"Jenny, why do you do this to me?"

Now the waitress and cooks were uncomfortable.

They shuffled away, leaving the Baked Alaska flaming in front of the couple.

"We've been playing this tug of war game for years," Michael said. "Let's end it once and for all. Be my wife already."

Jenny considered his proposition, and after a bit of playful thought, she said the word she knew in her heart she had wanted to say for decades. "Yes."

"Really?" Michael needed to confirm this was real.

"Let's do the dang thing," Jenny squealed.

Michael removed the old ring from Jenny's finger and replaced it with the new one.

"Here's to turning a new page," he said. In that moment, he felt as if he had won a race or conquered a city. He finally had the one thing money and prestige couldn't buy—Jenny, his tormented goddess.

They got home just before midnight. Michael selected a record from the bookshelf, and the scratch of the vinyl had a new sound to him. He took Jenny's hand and kissed the ring he had put on her finger not a couple of hours before. They swayed back and forth to the melody, and he twirled her around like they were at a high-school dance. The clock stuck midnight, and they kissed. "Happy 2018. I love you baby," Michael said.

"This year is our year," Jenny replied. She really did believe this would be their best year yet.

Within two months, Michael and Jenny arranged the wedding of their dreams. This time around, Jenny had family and friends to support her and hold the train of her stunningly gorgeous A-line dress. Michael didn't have to drink his way through this wedding, and remained sober through it all. He didn't want to forget one single moment.

It made Jenny's day seeing her mother and Michael's mother sitting in the front row beside Michael's kids. Dr. Scott, his wife, and their daughter attended too. Of course, Sarah stood next to her as the maid of honor, and everything was as perfect as Jenny had imagined.

As she slid into her wedding dress, alone in the ladies' room, she couldn't help but replay her first wedding. The police officers said he was dead; she had seen the picture, after all.

Sometimes, however, she could still almost feel his presence in the air. There would be a chill, a whisper, and she would feel heavier for an instant. She pushed aside the fear. Must be cold feet. Her mom came in to help her lace up the final threads of the corset, and she was ready to walk down the aisle.

To Michael, Jenny looked like an angel. As she glided toward him, he was propelled back to 1996 when they had just met, and he felt the butterflies all over again. The pastor led them through the ceremony and the pair exchanged *I dos*. Both of them cried, but Michael cried more. Jenny found it funny and endearing. They kissed while friends and family clapped in congratulations.

The next morning, Jenny rolled over to see Michael on the balcony. He was drinking his usual cup of black coffee, and Jenny realized just how much she really loved his routine. She shuffled the covers around, and Michael turned to check on her.

"Good morning, Mrs. Anderson." He pecked her forehead. "I've got a surprise in store for you."

He grabbed two plane tickets from his dresser drawer. "We're going to Italy soon. I want you to take me to all the places you visited when you were there."

Jenny could tell that Michael was trying to meet her halfway. He had never been much of a traveler, but he knew she loved it. And she appreciated his gesture.

"You will love everything there. It's like you're in a dream," she said.

A few days later, Michael and Jenny embarked on their dream honeymoon. The first stop on their itinerary was the lake she'd grown so fond of during her stay years ago.

She pointed to her bench. "This is where I sat for hours at a time and thought of you. Moving here proved to me how much I loved you. I knew from then on that I couldn't live without you." Since they were practically in the neighborhood, Jenny introduced Michael to her friends. Paula, her husband, and Ray were happy to see Jenny healthy and happy. They visited ancient Roman ruins, explored dilapidated bathhouses, and sipped fine wines on gondola rides throughout the city. When they returned home, they felt as if they'd crammed a lifetime of travel into a few weeks.

They had never been happier.

The fireflies began disappearing; a sure sign that summer was coming to its end in Michigan. A beaming Sunday morning sun illuminated Michael and Jenny as they caught a few more minutes of sleep. Michael's phone rang.

"Hey Jen, would you mind grabbing my phone?"

It was Christa. Jenny picked it up and handed it to him. Christa screamed through the speakers. She sounded distraught and was crying so hard, Jenny could barely make out what she was saying. She hung up and Michael stood, speechless.

"Uh, I have to go," he said. "My son is hurt. Some kind of accident. He's in the hospital. I'll call you when I know more." He threw on a band Tshirt and khaki pants and rushed away.

Michael arrived at the hospital and heard the news.

Car on bike. A hit and run. The boy was lucky to be alive. Christa fell to her knees as the doctor read off stats about her son's condition. None of it made sense to her, or to Michael, either.

"Don't cry," he said. "Everything will be all right."

A few hours passed. The doctor beckoned Christa and Michael from the waiting room. Their son would be okay. He needed rest and would have to be monitored over the next several days. Michael called Jenny.

"He's fine," Michael said. "But he has to stay in the hospital. I won't be home for a while."

For four days, Michael and Christa ate, drank, and slept by their son. Jenny felt useless, and she was concerned for her stepson. Hospitals could be so scary, so sterile and unwelcoming. She knew that life. Maybe she could help. She decided to make a visit.

Christa saw Jenny walk into her son's room, and she turned into a cartoon. You could practically see the steam billowing out of her ears. "What the fuck are you doing here?"

Michael shot up and rushed toward them with his hands spread apart, as if ready to position them between the two women.

"Shush, girls. The boy is asleep," he said in a low voice and lifted his finger to his lips.

"Can you give us a minute?" Jenny asked Michael. He nodded and exited the room, leaving her alone with Christa.

"I'm not here to encroach on anything. You've been here for several days, and I feel compelled to help. Please, consider letting me stay with the boy for a bit so you and Michael can go home and rest." Jenny hoped her sincerity would shine through and touch Christa's heart somehow.

"You want me to leave my son with you? Are you out of your mind?"

"I think I have something of value to share here," Jenny explained. "I know how you feel, how your son feels. I've spent half of my life in hospitals. They're terrible, but I know the ways to make them seem brighter."

Christa looked at her with equal parts amazement and skepticism.

"I care about your kids, Christa. I'm not the enemy. Today is a different day, and I think it's time we leave the past in the past. For the kids, for Michael, and for you."

The tension lifted, albeit, sparingly. Christa reached out for Jenny's hand and then pulled her into a long embrace.

"I'm sorry. I'm sorry for not giving you the benefit of the doubt." It was like she opened the floodgates and years of hate were spilling over the ceramic hospital floors.

Christa grabbed her purse from a chair and walked hand-in-hand with Jenny out of the room. Her eyes were red from the tears Jenny had inspired. Michael watched the two women with disbelief. Were they being cordial toward one another? Had something changed?

"I'm going home to rest and check on the kids," Christa said to Michael. "Jenny is staying here to watch over the boy."

Michael hugged Christa before she left and then stared at Jenny longingly.

"You always find a way to amaze me, Jenny."

"Go home and rest, too," she said. "I can hold down the fort here."

Michael kissed her and left. Jenny returned to the boy.

She grabbed a chair and sat by the bed. He was so small as he slept under the cold, fluorescent lights. His face and body were covered in dark bruises, like an overripe banana. She'd never been able to see him up close like this. He looked so much like his father. The similarities made Jenny smile and think of her dear Michael.

When he woke from his slumber a few hours later, he saw Jenny instead of Christa. Confused, he asked, "Where is mommy?"

"Hello there," Jenny said softly. "Mommy will be back soon; how do you feel?"

"Thirsty," he exclaimed. Jenny laughed and filled a glass up to the brim with water.

"Where's daddy?" he asked.

"He will be back soon, too," Jenny replied.

"Thanks, Jenny." It was just two, simple words, but they meant the world to Jenny.

She spent the whole night by the boy's bedside.

Christa and Michael arrived the next morning to a much happier and much healthier son. As the couple doted over their precious child and smothered him in hugs and kisses, Jenny watched in dismay. Seeing them so engulfed in parental bliss struck a chord, one that events of this nature had hit many times before. Jenny left the room, left mother and father to son.

Michael noticed her long, slow walk out of the hospital room. He could tell something wasn't right, and he was pretty sure he knew what it was. But at the moment, he was just happy his son had pulled through and survived the horrific accident.

A few days later, Michael's son was discharged.

Although the boy was better, Jenny felt uneasy. She began contemplating her future with Michael. Her desire was to have kids, but the cancer had made that more difficult.

Was she ready to endure more hospitals, more doctors? She didn't believe she was strong enough for that.

One day, she dipped her toes in the pool in her backyard. Michael watched her from afar. Her blank stare concerned him, but he knew what she was thinking about. Ever since his son's accident, Jenny had been wandering in the children's aisle of department stores and placing more framed pictures of his kids around the house. She wanted a baby, and he believed they could make it work.

"Jenny, what's wrong?"

"Nothing at all, my love. Just wading."

"Can I tell you a secret?"

She hesitated. "Sure."

"I know what you're thinking. I can read your mind."

He was playing a game, she thought. "Okay, okay. I'll bite. What am I thinking?" She giggled and punched his shoulder lightheartedly.

"You're thinking about babies and big families."

Her laughter ceased, and she got serious. "How did you know that?"

"I saw your face at the hospital with my son. I know having a child is important to you," Michael confessed. "I know it'll be hard, but let's try."

"I don't want to talk about it, Michael."

"No, look at me. We can do this." He cupped her hand in his. "There are lots of options, like invitro fertilization. I've already talked with Dr. Scott. He's in this with us one-hundred percent."

His enthusiasm brought tears to her eyes.

"Can we do it without hospitals and excessive treatments?"

"Maybe, Jenny. We'll have to see. Promise me you'll try? Come with me to a consultation. We'll figure it out."

She eventually agreed. *Maybe* wasn't *no.* She was interested to learn more.

After a few consultations, she felt prepared enough to begin treatments. "We'll see how this goes," she thought, "but if it doesn't work, I'll have to give up"

Michael's son, Corey, would be seven soon, and Jenny couldn't wait to host his birthday party. She went to the grocery store to buy ingredients for a themed cake she planned to attempt that afternoon.

The lady at the checkout counter saw the sprinkles, icing, and flour. "Someone's celebrating something special," she commented delightfully.

"It's my stepson's birthday," Jenny gushed. She enjoyed having kids and loved mentioning them to anyone, anywhere.

"Ooh, that's so exciting. Wish him a very happy birthday for me," the cashier said. "Will do."

Jenny pushed her cart away and toward her minivan. She was transferring her plastic bags of groceries from cart to trunk, when she was struck from behind. Her purse and a shopping bag fell to the ground. She felt the barrel of a gun pressed against her back.

An old, familiar voice spoke into her ear. "Is the goddess gonna have a party?" It was Richard. How could it be? Wasn't he dead?

She remembered the photo, the police officers. Hadn't she identified him and seen the bullet holes for herself?

"I thought you were dead."

He laughed. "Everyone does. Moss is dead. Drug deal gone bad. But I got his ID before he passed. It's covered my ass for years."

Richard forced Jenny into the driver's seat. From the passenger's seat, he pointed the gun and told her to drive. They took I-75 South all the way to Ohio.

"What's your game plan here?" Jenny asked him. She wasn't sure she would make it out of this alive, especially after the last time he'd kidnapped her. He'd torture her, and she'd suffer again.

"You'll find out soon enough," he said.

After many hours, they reached an abandoned plant just outside of Columbus. He grabbed her arm and led her inside the building.

He waved the gun around. "Did you miss me?"

"Please don't hurt me," she pleaded. "I will do whatever you want."

"I know you will. I've been watching you. You've gotten weak. Getting married to Michael, trying to have a baby, making stupid birthday cakes." He spit on the ground. "It's disgusting."

He motioned to a chair in the corner. She obeyed his command and sat. He wrapped thick rope around her arms and pushed his face against hers.

"You look so beautiful. It's too bad that you don't miss me." He bit her lip, and she recoiled like a spring.

"What do you want, Richard?"

"You. You are worth a fortune now, Mrs. Anderson.

I've seen the house you live in, the cars you and your husband drive. You seem to have done pretty well for yourself. I knew I'd be able to tap into your resources again. It was only a matter of time."

"Do you really think you will get away with this?

Michael is probably on his way right now." She sounded confident, but inside, she wasn't so sure.

"Ha! Michael. He's just as simple and weak as your beloved friend, Oliver. I can slice his throat too, you know."

Jenny connected the dots.

"You killed Oliver," she gasped. "You piece of shit." With her one free hand, she grabbed a metal post and barely scraped Richard's face. Taking the post from her, he proceeded to kick her repeatedly until she couldn't breathe.

"It's easy to slice a throat," he said. "I can do yours, too."

"Fuck you." She spit on his shoe.

"I always liked the way you resisted." He strolled toward her, bent down, and forced his lips onto hers. She bit him, and he responded with a swift punch to her face.

In Michigan, Michael was worried. In a few hours it would be nightfall, and Jenny wasn't answering her phone. He left the office and headed straight to the house. She would have to be there by now. As he turned the corner onto their street, his anxiety intensified. Jenny's car wasn't in the driveway. He knew she'd gone out to run a few errands, but she had never been out this long before. This was unusual and definitely out of character for his goddess.

"Hey," he said into his phone speaker, greeting Jenny's mom. "Is Jenny with you?"

"No. She isn't," she said. "Why do you ask?" "No reason. Just having trouble reaching her. She must be busy. Talk soon," Michael said, and ended the call. He didn't want to alarm Jenny's mom just yet.

That was strike one, he thought. Then he tried Sarah, but that too was without success. No one knew where his wife could have been with had seen or heard from her.

Michael reached for his phone and his finger hovered over the 9. As he prepared to dial 9-1-1, two police cars pulled into his driveway. He opened the door and met them outside. A commanding individual stepped out of the vehicle and approached Michael.

"Good afternoon, sir. I'm Agent McKinney, and I'm here to investigate a potential crime."

This sent Michael in a spiral. Another police officer staggered behind the first. Michael could hardly keep his head on straight, let alone align his thoughts for the conversation that was about to ensue. The second police officer held out a purse.

"We found this outside the supermarket near Bloomfield Hills," he said. Michael immediately recognized it. It was Jenny's. She didn't go anywhere without it. He opened it up to see the photo of her and his son during his last day in the hospital. The fear subsided, making way for anger.

"What's going on?"

"Earlier today, a couple people called in about a possible abduction. Both accounts mentioned seeing a woman with long dark hair get into a car with a suspect male. When we followed up on the tips, we found her purse. He must have surprised her, or maybe she dropped it on purpose in hopes that someone would find it. At this point, we don't know."

"So, what's next? Where's my wife? Why aren't you guys looking for her?" Michael was a wreck.

"Sir, calm down. We reviewed the video footage from the parking lot. We know a white male, about 5'8" forced her into her vehicle. Is there anyone in your life that matches that description, who may want to hurt your wife?"

Although he rattled his brain for an answer, no one came to mind. Who would ever want to harm his dear Jenny?

"It's okay," McKinney said. "We have her plates, and if they're still driving her vehicle, we can track it. The moment they cross state lines, we'll know."

Richard lifted a straw to Jenny's mouth and allowed her a two-second sip of water. He sat at a table across from her and folded his hands, as if they were in the middle of a business meeting, negotiating the terms of a big deal.

"Now, Jen, this is how it's gonna go," he asserted. "You are a precious asset. Michael wants you to return, right? He would do anything. So, we're going to conduct a swap. You for some cash.

Well, not *some* cash. A lot of cash, obviously." She looked down at her feet, speechless.

Richard was getting tired of her games. "Say something," he shouted.

Jenny slowly shifted her eyes upward and spit in his direction again.

"All right, you can choose to do this the hard way or the easy way. And baby, I suggest you take the easy way. I'm going to get my millions one way or another."

"You'll never get a dime," she said.

He grabbed her hand and brushed his finger across her ring. "I'll kill Michael if you don't do as I say."

"You wouldn't dare," she said.

"Then I will slaughter his kids one-by-one, while you watch." He knew she had a weak spot for children.

Jenny felt exposed like an open wound. "You are sick," she muttered.

"Five-million dollars, sweetheart. That'll free you and keep those stupid kids you care so much about safe."

"Fine," she said. "My credit cards are in my pocket.

I'll give you the PINs."

He wound up his leg like a spring and kicked her stomach. She yelped. He pulled a notebook out of a drawer in the warehouse and handed it and a pencil to her.

"Write down the PINs. They better be right."

After she gave the notebook back to him, he took the credit cards and her car keys and drove to a gas station. The nearest town was more than 20 miles away.

Hours had gone by, and there was no trace of Jenny. Michael stood over the policemen's shoulders, tuning into to every update and code that came through their handheld radios. No one knew anything, and he felt completely helpless. Who could have done this? Where was his dream girl? Had he already lost her again, and this time, would it be for good?

He heard a cacophony of noise behind him. The policemen were shuffling their gear and pacing the living room.

"They've spotted Jenny's car, somewhere around Columbus, Ohio," McKinney said to Michael.

Without thinking, Michael seized his handgun from a safe, got into his sports car, and whizzed away from his hometown. He sped like a maniac the whole way to Ohio, and when he was about twenty miles from Columbus, he stopped at a gas station to get his bearings. Upon stopping, he suddenly realized that he had no idea where to go from here. Crying, he fell asleep in his car.

Richard took the credit cards and a wad of cash he'd found under the dash of Jenny's car and bought a six-pack of beer and cigarettes. He needed to buy some time before connecting with Michael or the police, who he was sure were onto him by now. When Richard swiped the card at the gas station, Michael received a notification from his bank on his phone. It was a fraud alert, and it stirred him from his sleep.

Maybe it had to do with Jenny? He called the bank because it was worth a shot if the alert would somehow lead him to her. The customer service representative told him a transaction had been made an hour ago at a gas station in Ohio. She gave him the name of the place, and Michael was relieved. He had what he needed to find Jenny.

When he arrived at the gas station, he asked the clerk if he'd seen anyone driving Jenny's car. He provided the description, and to Michael's delight, the clerk remembered which direction it headed. Pointing south, the clerk gave him a general path to follow.

For the next several hours, he scoured the roads surrounding the gas station where his card had been used fraudulently. He explored old farmhouses and abandoned sheds. Nothing. Finally, he spotted a light coming from behind some hills and followed it, unsure of what he might uncover or encounter.

Michael drove cautiously along a gravel path. He parked hundreds of yards from the old warehouse so as not to alert the abductor if Jenny was in there. He heard a noise and saw a shadow, so he hopped behind a bush to conceal his presence. When he peeked above the lush brush, he saw a man grabbing beer out of the back of Jenny's car. It wasn't just any man. It was Richard. Jenny had said he was dead. She'd seen the photographs with her own two eyes. He quickly phoned the police with his new information.

They warned him to stay back, but even they knew that was a pointless request. Their only recourse was to follow him and get there before anything unfortunate happened.

It was clear now that Richard had used Moss's early demise to keep himself out of jail. He stole his I.D. and resumed life as his older brother for the past several years. Michael understood the gravity of the situation. Jenny was in real trouble here. Richard had beaten her to the brink of death before, and he would do it again if he hadn't already.

With his gun at the ready, Michael approached the abandoned warehouse. He could see Jenny's silhouette through the dirty glass window. She was alive. Michael found a cracked open door and slid through it as fast and quietly as he possibly could, and then he waited for the right time to make his move.

Jenny lay on the cement in pain. Her face was swollen and bruises the size of acorns covered her face. Her mouth gushed blood like a river during a flood.

Richard reviewed the plan with her. Tomorrow morning, they would contact Michael and get him to conduct the transfer. Jenny nodded her head. She didn't care how he got the money. She just wanted to keep her husband and family safe.

"Whatever," she said.

"You tired of plotting tonight, sweetheart?" He was condescending and unrelenting. And his words were laced with a desire she knew she wouldn't be able to keep much longer.

He grabbed her neck and lifted her an inch or more off the floor. Her feet dangled. After releasing her, he ripped her shirt. While he took his off, Jenny attempted to escape, crawling across the floor on her hands and knees, crying.

Michael couldn't stand it. He tiptoed around the banister, but withheld his anger to keep Jenny alive. As much as he hated seeing Richard force himself onto Jenny, the position would be compromising for the bastard, and Michael could use the element of surprise to stun him.

Jenny screamed. "Get off of me! leave me alone!"

"I've been waiting to touch your tight little body for years," he said. He unzipped his pants, and then he felt something hit his head.

Michael swiped him with the barrel of his gun, knocking him off Jenny. The pair tussled on top of each other until Michael gained the upper hand and pointed the gun at Richard's face. Michael didn't hesitate. He killed the son of a bitch on the spot.

Jenny shrieked. She'd never seen a person killed before. Michael rolled Richard face-down so Jenny wouldn't have to see the mess of membranes. He took her in his arms and shielded her face, guiding her toward the warehouse doors.

"Let's get out of here," he said. "It's over now; you're safe." He kissed her cheeks.

The police arrived and called ambulances to take Michael and Jenny to the ER for a routine check-up. Jenny had suffered psychological trauma, and Michael sat by her bed as she slept. It was such a relief to know that Richard was truly out of their lives. It felt like a brand- new day. But he knew this would shake Jenny for a while.

Jenny woke up, confused. In her mind, she was still tied up and in the warehouse with Richard.

"No, stop! Let me go! Stop!"

Michael held her arms. "Baby, you're okay. Richard is gone. It's me, Michael."

"I'm so sorry this happened," Jenny cried. "I cause you so much trouble. How do you put up with me?"

"This was not your fault," Michael replied. "Don't for one second think it was. I only care that you're safe. Nothing else matters."

"I put you and your kids in danger," she said. "How can you forgive me for that?"

"Some things are outside of our control, Jenny. You could not possibly have known Richard would do this. I used to think I could control you, make you love me even when you weren't ready. I've learned a lot from this experience."

Jenny noticed a change in Michael. He finally got her, and she, well, she finally got him.

"I've never really deserved you," Jenny said. "But I'm glad you were here. You've always been here, haven't you?"

They kissed and watched the sunrise from Jenny's hospital-room window.

A run-in with Richard wasn't exactly what Jenny had needed. She'd been going through treatments as she and Michael attempted to have a child. Michael knew she was struggling, and so he went into the office late and came back home early. He wanted to be there for her as often as possible. He accompanied her to every clinic visit and held her hand through procedures and check-ups.

Within a few months, she received the answer she'd been praying for, but never really thought she'd get. The treatments had worked. She and Michael had conceived. They would have a baby. After all of the bad the couple had endured, she was grateful for this enormous gift of good.

Jenny hadn't seen Christa in months. Michael's ex-wife had taken some time for herself to do the things she'd neglected while married to him. It was Michael's weekend with the kids, and Christa brought them to Jenny's house. Jenny opened the door, and Christa was greeted to the sight of her billowing belly.

"Oh my," she exclaimed. "Pregnant?" "Yes." Jenny glowed.

"I'm sorry. Michael must not have mentioned it. Congratulations! But honestly, I would have called the kids' nanny if I had known."

"No need," Jenny said. "I can still take care of them. I wouldn't turn down the time for a second." "Is it a boy or a girl?" Christa asked.

Jenny told her about the most recent ultrasound and how she and Michael discovered they were having a boy.

"Having a child is such a delight," Christa said. "I would be more than happy to help with the baby shower and whatever you need. You can call on me. Really."

The new life growing inside Jenny began a new chapter for her and Christa. Perhaps it was possible for them to bury the hatchet and start over.

"That would be wonderful. And likewise, of course, with your kids. They can come over anytime," Jenny said.

Christa and Jenny hugged each other. The air felt a little lighter and the sun a little brighter. Change was coming, and Jenny was thankful for that.

Later that afternoon, Michael returned from work to see Jenny playing in the pool with his kids. He smiled and thought about how this was the happiest he had ever been.

Jenny looked up from her seat by the pool. "Daddy's here."

"How's your day been?" he asked her. "Just perfect," Jenny said. "And yours?"

He turned his head to the side and smiled. "Great, especially after coming home to this. You, the kids, our baby. I never expected things to work out the way they did."

"I guess we really can't control everything, huh?" Jenny and Michael held hands and leaped into the pool, while water splashed in all directions.

I hope you enjoyed reading Twenty-One Years. It would be great if you'd go to amazon.com and leave a review. I'd like to know what you thought of the story.

You can learn more about me and upcoming books on my website: geealtaee.com.

www.ingramcontent.com/pod-product-compliance
Lightning Source LLC
Chambersburg PA
CBHW072353110726
47909CB00003B/692